7-08

LOST WOLF RIVER

**Center Point
Large Print**

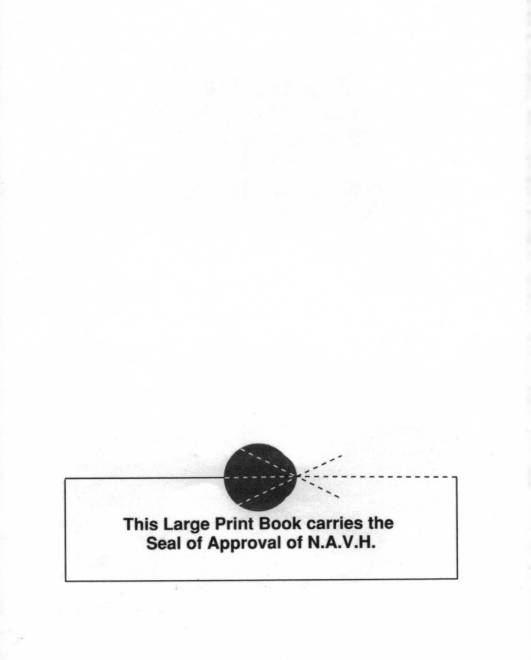

**This Large Print Book carries the
Seal of Approval of N.A.V.H.**

LOST WOLF RIVER

D. B. Newton

CENTER POINT PUBLISHING
THORNDIKE, MAINE

This Center Point Large Print edition
is published in the year 2008 by arrangement with
Golden West Literary Agency.

Copyright © 1952 by D. B. Newton.
Copyright © renewed 1980 by D. B. Newton.

The text of this Large Print edition is unabridged. In other
aspects, this book may vary from the original edition.
Printed in the United States of America.
Set in 16-point Times New Roman type.

ISBN: 978-1-60285-216-7

Library of Congress Cataloging-in-Publication Data

Newton, D. B. (Dwight Bennett), 1916-
    Lost Wolf River / D. B. Newton.--Center Point large print ed.
        p. cm.
    ISBN-13: 978-1-60285-216-7 (lib. bdg. : alk. paper)
    1. Large type books. I. Title.

PS3527.E9178L67 2008
813'.54--dc22

2008004908

ONE

The cowboy's name was Chick Bronson, and he was down on his luck—way, way down. Only twenty-five, he'd already been on his own for ten long years; but this one was turning out to be the toughest year of them all.

Since early spring, when panic hit the eastern beef markets, he had been following the forlorn gleam of possible jobs from one busted range to another, clear across the cow country—seldom finding anything, at most not able to stick anywhere longer than a week or two. Now here it was fall again, with winter looming not too far ahead; and normally resilient spirits, that had enabled him to bounce back many times in the past, had just about worn out all their bounce.

The day Chick Bronson trailed into this town of Hondo Forks he was very close to being exactly what he looked—a beaten, shabby figure, with unrewarded hopes dragging at the line of his shoulders.

He lagged slowly in across the deep dust of the courthouse square, put his gaunted sorrel to a hitch pole, and swung down. Tying, he used a lot of time fiddling with the knot, his hungry stare, meanwhile, sizing up the place in the desperate intentness of one who knows he has got to do something and yet has no clear idea what it's going to be.

Hondo Forks showed no more evidence of friendship toward a jobless stranger than any of the other towns. Almost no saddle horses or ranch rigs stood at the tie poles around the square, and that was a bad sign; it meant little buying in the stores, little business activity. It meant even normally generous folk would be hard to approach.

Then painted letters on a dusty saloon window caught and held his attention: FREE LUNCH. That was a misnomer, of course. Lunch was free only if you had the price of a drink in your jeans. Still, it gave Chick Bronson what he saw to be his only likely chance; and, pausing long enough to bat some of the thick dust out of his clothing, he swung under the pole and went directly across the warped sidewalk plankings.

Before entering, though, he hesitated a moment, gathering his courage, one hand on the batwing panels; it was thus he noticed the frayed poster tacked up against the clapboards, He'd run across others like it in his wanderings and knew the block of printing by heart. A thousand dollars for the capture and conviction of one Ward McCarey. . . . Yes, there was a man who had his own way of solving the money problem. Fifty thousand taken, they said, in this last bank job at Three Pines a week ago. Yet Chick Bronson did not really envy him.

A man could be pretty broke and still not feel the urge to steal, or the willingness to beg for it, either. There was still pride in Chick Bronson and a basic honesty and need for self-respect.

He walked into the saloon, and the first sour, damp smell of the place hit him hard in his empty belly.

It was a big place—the biggest in Hondo Forks, and probably doing more business than the other three added together. The brass footrail fronting the long bar was kept to a high polish by constant contact with boot leather, and the mirror of the back bar reflected a colorful array of varied liquors in pyramided bottles. The big room held space for a good number of tables and for gambling devices of numerous kinds. There was a cleared area for dancing and a small stage with kerosene footlights.

All this bespoke a good income for the proprietor, for however broke a range might be otherwise, you knew it would always have money to spend in places such as this, to help swamp its worries.

At the moment the saloon was nearly empty. A small knot of men were clustered around a pool table at the dark rear of the room, under the cone of light from an overhead lamp; grunted comments and the click of cues on ivory were the only sounds that greeted Chick Bronson's unobtrusive entrance. A bartender on duty was refilling a lamp for a wall bracket behind the counter and did not so much as glance up from his work as Chick crossed the spur-marked floor and placed a hand on the edge of the bar.

Chick Bronson cleared his throat. "I haven't got any money—" he began.

The aprons shot him the briefest of looks. "Then get out!"

He swallowed the curt answer. Indignation was one of the luxuries he could not afford.

7

"I'm not a deadbeat," he persisted. "Or a barfly, either. It's not a drink I want. I am near starved!" He pointed to the free lunch—a platter holding stacks of sliced bread and meat, a bowl of hard-boiled eggs, a jar of pickles. "I thought maybe, in return for letting me fix myself a sandwich, there'd be some odd jobs I could do. I could swamp out the place, or wash glasses, or fill the rest of these lamps for you."

"What you can do," the aprons said harshly, "is get the hell out of here. Ott Stanger don't allow no bums on the premises."

"But"—an angry flush had started crowding up through Chick Bronson's neck, touching sun-darkened cheeks, smoking up his gray-blue eyes—"it isn't a handout I'm asking for. I just want a chance to earn some grub."

"You heard me!" One big hand moved out of sight beneath the counter, where the barkeep undoubtedly kept a bung starter. "Now beat it before I flatten your ears into your skull!"

A new voice demanded sharply, "What's wrong here?"

The argument had carried to the pool table at the rear of the room, and some of the men were moving forward. In the van was one whose greedy arrogance showed in the very cut of the clothing he wore, in the cool contempt of the stare he placed upon Chick Bronson. Chick surmised with one glance that this was the owner of the saloon, Ott Stanger himself, and he pegged the big, animal-like shape looming at his elbow as probably being Stanger's bouncer and bodyguard. He knew all at once he had walked into something here that he had never bargained for.

But stubbornness was rising in him. He held his ground.

The barkeep had his bung starter in view now, tapping it gently against the edge of the bar. He growled, "Another of them damned panhandlers, Mr. Stanger. You said the next one that dared stick his nose inside those doors would get the full treatment."

Chick's right hand had lifted close to the gap of his brush jacket, close to the rubber-butted six-gun thrust behind his jeans waistband. "You don't call me a panhandler or a bum either!" he retorted hotly. "I came in offering to work for a bait of grub, and I'll do anything within reason to earn it. It's not my fault I haven't got any money in my pocket."

"Any man without money in his pocket is a bum," retorted Ott Stanger contemptuously. "And there seem to be more of them every day. I think it's time I made an example to keep the rest of 'em out of here."

At that Chick Bronson boiled over. "Why, you damned, sanctimonious—"

Stanger threw an order from the side of his mouth, flatly. "Take him, Dugan!"

The gorilla shoved past, starting for Chick with hands spread and an eager desire to hurt shaping his ugly, broadnosed face. He was nearly a head taller than the stranger, and with slabby strength to break any slighter man in two if those groping, thick-fingered hands could reach him.

But Chick Bronson had no desire to let this happen. He stumbled back a step, pawing at the tail of his coat. Then he had the six-gun cleared, and he whipped it forward, dropping its long barrel against the man closing in.

Awkward as the draw had been, it caught everyone by surprise. Dugan stopped in his tracks, grunting sharply; the rest of them stared at the stranger and his gun, and though all were armed they did not make any effort to reach for weapons of their own.

Rage conspired with hunger weakness to make Chick Bronson's arm tremble under the weight of the leveled Colt, but he held it steady. His facial muscles felt like a stiff, plated mask drawn tight across his skull. He gritted, "Any man who'd let another starve, and set his bully-boy on him . . ." Disgust blocked his speech, choking him, and he finished with a shrug of hunched shoulders. "Aw, hell! Why try to talk decency into someone that ain't got any?"

There was nothing to do but get out of there. At his elbow was the pile of free lunch materials, and sight of the food was a temptation that had him almost ready to reach for a handful of it to cram into his watering mouth. And yet he knew he dared not. He was in bad enough trouble already, and if he added the stealing of a single slice of stale bread and meat from Ott Stanger's free lunch, there was no telling what the saloon man might make of it.

Yes, that half-mythical gent on the reward notice outside—that Ward McCarey—could help himself to fifty thousand dollars from a bank till and get away with it. Yet Chick Bronson could not even take a few bites of food for his starved gut. That was how it went. . . .

It was in this instant that the aprons threw his bung starter.

Chick Bronson saw the motion from the tail of his eye and ducked, letting the crude weapon go end for end above his head, so close that he almost felt the wind of its passage. And thrown off balance like that, and helpless, he gave big Dugan the chance he wanted. The bouncer waded forward; he knocked aside the gun that Chick tried desperately to bring up into line again. Chick struck, wildly, and his fist bounced off the man's thick arm without any sting behind it.

Then Dugan's clubbed fist descended in a short and chopping blow. There was no chance of ducking it, as he had done to the bung starter. It came down, and Chick Bronson thought a mountain had collapsed upon the back of his neck. He rode the avalanche into darkness and a bottomless pit.

His next awareness was of eye-punishing daylight crossed by bars of shadow—the iron window bars of Hondo Forks jail. . . .

TWO

On a flat store roof across the way a man sat motionless, shotgun on knees, and chain-smoking one hand-rolled cigarette after another. A second guard had been posted under the shade of a feed-store awning, some ten yards farther along; and though Chick Bronson hadn't noticed them when he rode in, and couldn't see them from this window, he suspected that still others lined the remaining three sides of the dusty square.

Listening to the scratch of the jailer's blunt pen point, he wondered dully what such precautions could be about. Surely, he knew, they weren't just on his account!

The door wrenched open suddenly and the sheriff tramped in, booted it shut behind him. He was a heavy man, with a powerful dark mustache and a scowl that shadowed his eyes as he looked at his prisoner. He said to the jailer, "Got him booked?"

"Yeah." The man jerked a thumb at a pile of personal belongings on the corner of the desk. "There's what I took off him. I'm makin' out the receipt."

The lawman looked at the pile, stirred it with a blunt-fingered hand. It didn't amount to much—a dirty handkerchief, a horn-handled clasp knife, the old rubber-butted six-gun together with a few extra shells, a mouth organ that had lost one of its back plates.

"No money at all, huh?" The sheriff considered this a moment; then, abruptly, turned to the prisoner. "All right," he commanded. "Strip!"

Chick Bronson straightened a little in his chair, blinking. "Do what?"

"You heard me! Get busy and start takin' 'em off— right down to the underwear!"

At another time he might have protested, but these last terrible months had taken too much out of him. Moving stiffly, because of the neck that still ached from Dugan's clubbing blow, Chick proceeded to disrobe. And as he did so, the sheriff seized each garment in turn and made his quick examination.

He ran the seams of the denim jacket through his fingers, probed each of the down-at-heels scuffed boots, and even the cuffs of the threadbare jeans. He pulled out the sweatband of the shapeless hat. Finally satisfied, he tossed all the clothing in a heap in front of the prisoner.

"Get into them again," he ordered curtly. To the jailer he added, "It's safe, I reckon—he's nothin' more than the saddle tramp he looks to be. Go ahead, lock him up, but as far from McCarey's cell as possible."

The jailer nodded, and hitching to his feet gathered the prisoner's belongings off the desk and dumped them in a drawer of a file case against the wall. He got a ring of keys from the desk drawer, then picked up the receipt he had been filling out and looked over at Chick.

Scowling, the latter had started dragging on his clothes again. With a yank at his jeans belt he turned on the sheriff. "Look!" he began, making a last try. "You got nothing on me, mister. Whatever those men in the saloon said, it's a lie. All I ever wanted—"

"Save it!" the lawman cut in harshly. "We'll talk it over later on, kid, when I haven't got so many things on my mind. Right now there's a charge against you of vagrancy and disturbing the peace. You'll get free meals for a few days and a place to flop. What is there to kick about?"

"But I tell you I'm no vag! I'm a top-hand cow poke! Just try me! Give me a chance at a job—any job—"

"I said we'll talk later! Now do as you're told. Take the clothes along with you; you can finish dressing in a cell."

Not listening to any more, the sheriff turned on his heel and strode out. Yonder, the jailer was swinging his keys impatiently. With a gun strapped to his waist, he looked in no mood to take an argument.

Chick shrugged resignedly and gathered up the rest of his clothing. A steel door led to the cell room behind the jail office. It opened to the stab of one of the big keys, and then the jailer stood aside and motioned Chick ahead of him. The whisper of the gun sliding out of leather into his hand, as a precaution, was plain in the stillness.

There were a half-dozen cells, three on either side of the stone-floored corridor, splitting the middle of the room. Chick's jailer stopped him at the first barred door, and as he stepped inside the cubicle the door slammed to behind him and the key turned.

"Look," Chick demanded suddenly, "what about my bronc?"

"We'll see to him. Now take this receipt and shut up!" The paper was shoved at him through the bars. And a moment later the man had gone and the big door clanged shut again.

For a long time Chick stood motionless, holding an armload of clothing and looking about at the dingy cell with its high window and its single bunk, its musty reek of stale mop water. From outside came the normal sounds of a cow town—the sing of spurs along boardwalk plankings, the clang of a blacksmith's anvil, the rattle of a passing ranch wagon.

Chick padded over in stocking feet and dumped his stuff onto the bunk. He had just sat down to pull on a boot when an eager whisper sounded through the silence.

"Who is it? That you, Cinco?"

He frowned, not understanding. "My name's Chick Bronson," he answered.

"Oh?" The voice sounded disappointed, completely set back for an instant. "But—somebody sent you, didn't they?"

"Nobody I know of—except the sheriff and that tough saloon-keeper across the street—" Suddenly a flash of light struck him. "Hey! It must be on account of you—having those guards posted, and searching me down to the hide this way before they threw me in! It's *you* they're scared might get away from them. Or that your friends might try to break you loose."

Then the name the sheriff had spoken struck him with delayed impact. "McCarey! Hell's bells! You're *Ward* McCarey! I hadn't heard nothing about you being caught. . . ."

"Shut up!" growled the voice, heavy with bitter disappointment.

Very thoughtfully Chick Bronson pulled on the rest of his clothing. To think of the legendary badman, captured, and his fellow prisoner! He peered through

15

the bars, trying hard to see along the corridor and deciding they must have McCarey down at the far end, where he couldn't look into the other cell. So after a bit Chick returned to his bunk and stretched out on the thin mattress to think about this, easing the soreness of a battered body and using his wadded brush jacket for a pillow.

There was a dull aching in his head still. That and the continuing emptiness of his belly and the bad air of the cell block put a touch of nausea inside him.

Such small stretch of sky as he could see beyond the window bars and the false fronts of neighboring buildings had turned pale with coming evening before the jailer unlocked the bull pen again. This time he actually brought food, that he shoved through the opening at the bottom of each cell door.

A plate of beef stew apiece, a chunk of bread, and coffee. Chick Bronson grabbed his eagerly; it was not bad grub to a man who had gone this long without. He was already tying into it before the jailer had reached that other cell at the end of the corridor.

He listened to them talking down there. He heard the jailer saying in a pleased tone, "Well, McCarey! We've got word from Three Pines. Their sheriff will be here sometime tomorrow to take you back, and he's bringing an army with him. Meanwhile, we're doubling the guard overnight, so I don't think anybody will have any luck breaking you loose. No, the law has got you this time, and you're going to take your medicine!"

16

Ward McCarey grunted something that got him a sadistic chuckle in reply. "By the way," the turnkey added, "how about the fifty thousand? How about letting a gent in on where you cached it, huh? You know you ain't going to be able to spend that money!"

"Go to hell!" said McCarey.

"If I do, you'll be there ahead of me. Oh yes, that's something I guess I forgot to mention! The bank teller you shot—he finally died! So you see it's a murder charge you'll be goin' back to!"

He came down the aisle after that with a jaunty whistle, swinging his keys; he clanged the door behind him.

Chick meanwhile had finished supper, to the last crumb of bread, and settled back feeling better than he had in days. A full stomach can work wonders for a man. He was suddenly not even worried about what the sheriff would do to him; a few weeks of free grub on the county seemed like the most, whatever that tough saloon owner across the street might have to say about it.

And here he was with a bed of sorts to sleep in and the prospect of breakfast in the morning. Now, if they had only let him keep his mouth organ to help spell the time he would really have had little to ask for.

The weight of warm food in his stomach made him dull with sleep. He stretched out comfortably on the bunk, letting the darkness gather, getting the tang of sage and heated rangeland that came to him with evening's stirring breath.

Down in that other cell he was dimly aware of the scrape of boots; they turned sharp at every third step, swinging back and forth across the narrow space—like the pacing of a caged animal, he thought drowsily. . . .

"Kid! Hey, kid—you awake?"

McCarey's whisper, echoing along the corridor, broke in upon Chick Bronson's doze and slowly roused him. He blinked into the darkness, saw the striped pattern of moonlight thrown by the high window upon the floor beside his bunk. He mumbled, "Yeah? What do you want?"

"Oh—nothin', really. But if you're awake I thought maybe you'd talk to me. Makes a guy restless just sitting here—waiting!"

Chick thought he understood, and his understanding startled him. "Getting scared, McCarey?"

"Scared? Me?" The outlaw's retort was scornful. But next instant his entire manner changed and he admitted in a different tone, "I guess you're right, fellow! Funny how a gent goes along, getting the breaks, and never really believing that everything can ball up at the last minute and hit him—right in the face. Hell, yes, I'm scared!"

"Have you given up hope of your friends?"

"Nobody can do what ain't possible. I got a lot of friends, but this sheriff is being too careful for them. They aren't going to get me away from him, I know that now. I'm going back to Three Pines tomorrow and stand trial—for murder!"

His voice choked a little on that word, and then he cried hoarsely, "Why did the damn fool have to try for a gun? Why did he make me plug him? In five years I never killed a man. And now, for this one time, when I was forced to it, I'm going to swing!"

Listening, Chick began to feel a sudden stirring of pity—odd enough, in a man who had lately fallen into the habit of considering himself about as pitiable as any grub-line-riding cow poke could get.

"Come on, kid!" Ward McCarey burst in on his thoughts, and he was almost pleading. "Just talk to me, will you?"

"What about?"

"I don't give a damn! Your life story—anything. How you come to wind up in this rotten hole?"

That was easy enough to do, and Chick Bronson told the miserable tale, glad enough at having an audience for his grievance against Ott Stanger and the bullying Dugan. McCarey heard him out.

"Yeah, that was tough," the outlaw agreed. After-ward there was a little silence. Chick felt the drowsiness begin to creep up on him again.

"You ain't quitting on me, are you?" Ward McCarey called plaintively. "It kind of helps, having something to listen to beside a man's own thoughts. Tell me more about yourself. Where'd you come from?"

"Away back, you mean? The Missouri Ozarks. My folks had a farm there, just outside Springfield."

McCarey said self-pityingly, "I never had no folks that I remember. I might of ended up different if I did.

All I had was an uncle that got drunk every week end and stripped the hide off me, until I was old enough to run away."

"My folks were good enough to me," Chick opined. "But scrub-oak land soured me early on farming. You can't grow nothing but rocks on them Ozark sidehills. I stuck it out until I was near fifteen, and then I come West. I ain't been back."

"Go on," Ward McCarey prompted him. "Tell me about your maw. What was she like?"

And because he could sense the desperate loneliness of this unseen stranger in the other cell, Chick Bronson tried to satisfy him. Hands laced behind his head, legs crossed and one boot waggling slowly, he stared at the dark ceiling and called those distant days to mind. He went deeper into memory than he had done in many a long month, dredging up the little, half-forgotten incidents of home life and spinning them out while the lassitude of sleep stole up on him again.

Like many an outlaw, Ward McCarey had a sur-prising streak of sentimentality about him. These tales of a kind of boyhood he had missed—the mere sound of Chick's droning voice—seemed to please him and soothe his tormented nerves. Every once in a while he would ask some question that showed he was fol-lowing avidly every word the other spoke.

Still, drowsiness eventually won out. Thoughts and sentences began to fall to pieces, and finally, without being aware how the transition had been made, Chick

20

no longer was talking about those remembered scenes but asleep instead and dreaming them. Nor did any sound come from that other cell to rouse him before gray streaks of dawn light began to filter through the bleak cell room, and Chick woke again, and for a moment was hard put to it remembering just where he was and how he came to be there.

His fellow prisoner's heavy breathing, still deep with slumber, rasped across the quiet of that cow-town jailhouse.

THREE

Sometime toward midmorning they came for Ward McCarey.

It was a regular armed squad that filed into the bull pen. In addition to the local sheriff and the jailer, a bunch of trail-dusty men followed a hard-bitten character whose badge proclaimed him to be the lawman from the neighboring county seat of Three Pines. Chick watched at the door of his own cell while they paraded past, spurs ajingle and gun harness creaking, and more than one of the sheriff's escort, he saw, carrying shotguns and saddle weapons openly.

"All right, McCarey," he heard the Three Pines lawman grunt with savage pleasure. "Let's go! There's a noose waitin' for you, and no use thinkin' you can pull any funny stuff to cheat it!"

The jailer's key unlocked the cell, there were a few moments of delay and murmured comments, and after

21

that the procession was coming in a ragged rhythm of boots along the narrow corridor. Chick Bronson watched, curious for a glimpse of the outlaw. It surprised him a little when he finally singled McCarey out.

He saw a big, well-built fellow with sandy mustache and a flowing mane of reddish hair. None of these others was exactly a small man, but McCarey topped them all. And when he came abreast of Chick's cell he suddenly halted, and the angry nudge of a gun against his ribs failed to budge him.

"Cut it out!" he growled. "You got all the time in the world to hang me in. Lemme have one minute to say a word to this kid, will you?" And, not waiting for an answer, he turned toward the bars and thrust a hand through them—his left, Chick noticed, for McCarey's right arm was strapped to his side in a dirty sling, apparently broken; it looked as though he hadn't been taken without a fight.

"So long, kid," McCarey grunted. "Thanks for keeping me company. You helped me through a bad night. Don't let these galoots get you down!"

"I won't," mumbled Chick, and reached to take the offered hand. "Keep your own chin up, McCarey."

He couldn't help the flickering of astonishment that passed over his face then as their palms met; but McCarey was turning away abruptly and hurling his heavy voice at those who guarded him. "All right, you damn' law dogs—let's go, if you're in such a hurry!" And maybe, Chick thought, no one had noticed, after all . . .

22

He waited until the men were gone, the steel door shut and locked again. Only then did he look at the thing Ward McCarey had left in his fingers.

There was a scrap of paper, and folded inside it a single silver dollar. The coin was badly battered and misshapen, with a shimmer of brightness near the hollowed center where some small but powerful missile must once have struck a smashing blow. Turning it over in his fingers, Chick saw that the outlaw's initials, "W.M.," had been scratched onto both its faces.

After staring at this a moment he smoothed out the paper and saw the writing. Apparently McCarey had scribbled the note that morning while waiting for the Three Pines sheriff and had kept it and the coin palmed until he had the chance to slip it through the bars to the other prisoner. The left-handed writing was hard to decipher, but he worked it out with growing wonder.

Kid, this is my lucky dollar. It stopped a bullet once that had my name written on it, and the worst I got was a couple of broken ribs. But it looks now like the luck must of ran out of it as far as I'm concerned. Maybe it will work better for you.

If you ever get over toward Lost Wolf River, show this coin to Vince Kimbrough. He'll recognize it, and if you need any help he'll give you some. Stand you a square or get you a job maybe. Vince was always a good friend of mine.

Such was the note; and something seemed to choke up inside Chick Bronson as he read the crude scrawl. Superstitious as any outlaw, Ward McCarey had nevertheless yielded up his precious lucky piece to help an unknown youngster who had befriended him. It didn't seem right, somehow, to take it.

Or maybe McCarey really felt, with a fatalistic conviction, that such power for his own good fortune as it had ever held was indeed run out, and that no charm could save him now from the rocky road that must end, inevitably, under the gallows in Three Pines.

Chick swallowed hard, and his hand tightened on the battered coin. Suddenly he knew that, overnight, he had formed a strange liking for the big, sentimental outlaw. And he knew also, with a grim certainty, that he would never see Ward McCarey again.

This was a dead man's dollar that he gripped within his sweating palm. . . .

It was past noon the next time anyone came near him. Chick Bronson had got hungry again, and he hoped they were bringing his dinner, but the jailer's hands were empty except for the key ring. Chick watched dumbly while his cell was unlocked and the door swung wide. "Step out!" he was ordered. "Sheriff wants to talk to you." And he thought the sour-faced man gave him a peculiar look as he shuffled past.

Seated with spurs hooked into the top of his desk, the sheriff was using a pocketknife to pare the nails of broad, splayed-fingered hands. He looked up with a scowl.

24

"Chick Bronson, huh?"

"Yeah."

The other pursed his lips, the ends of the mustache sticking straight forward as he did so, and fiddled with the knife. A fly droned against the window in the heated quiet of the stuffy jail office.

"I'm purely uncertain what should be done about you," grunted the lawman finally. He snapped the knife shut, unhooked his spurs, and swung his swivel chair around. "It all hangs on Ott Stanger. If he cares to make an issue out of it I'd say you'll probably end up with a term for vagrancy."

Chick insisted doggedly, "I told you before, I'm not a vag. I'd be glad to take a job if I could find one, but the outfits just ain't hiring. There's so many grub-liners going the rounds now they run you off with a shotgun when you ride in the gate!"

"Yeah, I understand times are bad. Somebody in Wall Street plays the wrong card and the cattlemen lose their shirts. No telling when things are apt to pick up, either."

The lawman scrubbed his grizzled head. "I reckon I understand about that doin's over at the saloon yesterday too. Stanger is a pretty hard character. To him, any man without a clean shirt and money to jingle is a bum and he won't allow him on the place."

"How could I be expected to know that? I was a stranger and thought maybe I could earn a meal. I never intended to start trouble—and I didn't, either! It was him and that tough bouncer he calls Dugan."

The sheriff made a face. "I can believe it!" He shrugged. "I'll tell you what, kid. I don't want to get tough with you. There's enough big-time crooks, like that McCarey we got rid of this morning, to keep a man busy without picking on every drifter that's down on his luck.

"So I'm gonna turn you out—but I mean *clear* out. I don't want you still around an hour from now, because if Ott Stanger sees you're loose he's sure to make trouble—for both of us!"

"Don't worry! I ain't aiming to tangle with him again. And there's nothing else to hold me in this town!"

"You got any plans at all?"

Chick fingered the battered dollar in his pocket. "Not for certain. But there's just a chance I might be able to promote something over on the Lost Wolf. A job, maybe. I got sort of a line on it."

"Oh. Well, that country's not in my bailiwick. Anyway, I wish you luck."

The sheriff pushed back his chair across splintered floor boards. "I'll get your stuff for you. That bonebag you call a horse is in the county corral, eating his damned head off. Quicker you take him off my hands the better I'll like it."

"You won't like it any better'n I will."

The clean tang of fall sunshine and fresh air against his face was good after the jail. He stood for a long moment with hat in hand, savoring it. But there were eighty miles to cover, or thereabouts, to Lost Wolf River and the possibility of a job and grub, and it looked as though he was scheduled to miss another meal. Determined to waste no time hitting the trail, he took up the slack in his belt and went hunting for the county corral.

It didn't appear to him as though the sorrel had been gorging himself any on the sheriff's grain. He looked every bit as gaunt as he had before—droopheaded and miserable, peering at Chick through the tooth-gnawed bars. Yet he managed to dig up a whicker of greeting from somewhere, and Chick, touched, gave the bony neck a grateful slap.

"My first pay," he promised solemnly, "if I ever do land another job, you draw a feed that'll put an inch-thick layer of fat across all them ribs of yours. You'll have oats running outa your ears!"

Minutes later he was leaving this town as inconspic-uously as he'd entered it, a scarecrow figure with empty pockets and with rundown clothing and gear, and no apparent future ahead of him.

Though it was a late season the sun still held con-siderable of its summer heat; sometimes a rider could sweat as much in October as in the heart of July. He traveled westward through sandy, red-soiled country that became bunched and crumpled as the near hills took shape on the horizon. It was new range to him, but he had asked questions; he knew the empty trail he followed would skirt those timber ridges, keeping them to his right as he swung south and west toward the valley of the Lost Wolf.

Some nice grass down that way, he had heard, with

a number of small-tally outfits working it as well as one or two big-size spreads. Not that he held out much hope any longer for a riding job anywhere. He'd been willing to wash glasses in the saloon back yonder for a meal. If this friend of Ward McCarey—this Vince Kimbrough—would offer him any kind of job at all, Chick knew he'd take it. Even though Kimbrough ran a livery stable and was looking for someone to shovel it out twice a day.

Toward sunset he had, for once, a piece of luck. He knocked over a jack rabbit—spilled it running with a snap shot from the back of his sorrel and saw it flop lifeless in a little puff of reddish dust. This was good shooting for Chick Bronson, who had no more than the working cowhand's proficiency with a six-gun and generally did little good against a moving target unless his own feet were solid on the ground. But he made a clean shot this time that took the jack's head off its shoulders and left the rest of it unmangled; and then and there Chick decided to make camp and cook him a meal.

Tough and stringy as the meat promised to be, it removed the pressure of trying to reach his destination tonight. Meanwhile, he had handy a sheltered spot at the foot of a pine-clad hill spur, with grass for the sorrel and a trickle of seep water and plenty of scattered down-timber branches to keep a fire going. But, most important, he had food; and his belly threatened to collapse against his backbone at the thought of any delay in getting at it.

So he offsaddled, picketed the sorrel, and gathered the makings for a small fire. He dismembered the jack with his case knife, skewered the sections on sharpened twigs, and set these in a circle about the tiny blaze. And, that done, leaned back in comfort against a log to keep an eye on his cooking.

Flames danced and crackled; the seep spring trickled musically in early darkness; the white-stockinged sorrel pulled at grass near by among the pines. Chick Bronson looked up at the stars that were coming out now in a darkening sky and at the gently rocking tree heads above; and, remembering what night in the jail had been like, he knew a sudden peace at the contrast between that and his present freedom. He dragged a deep breath of the piney air that blew against him.

Somewhere to his left a twig snapped.

He heard the sound plainly, but for a moment its warning failed to register, then he saw that his sorrel had left off grazing and, with lifted head, was staring past him into the shadows. Belatedly Chick Bronson realized the possible meaning of these things. He started to twist about for a look, and that was when the harsh voice at the edge of the trees said sharply, "Careful, fellow. There's two guns here. Leave yours alone and sit easy!"

Slowly he came around, and, in that awkward and helpless position, stared numbly at the half-seen figures that were only black and formless shapes in the darkness. They moved forward now, deliberately.

Firelight picked a metallic glint from a leveled hand gun, and then the face above it swam into gradual clearness.

Chick Bronson blinked, stupefied. Because the last thing he would have expected to see out here in this wilderness was the cruel and predatory face of the saloon man, Ott Stanger.

FOUR

Stammering something, he scrambled to his feet. Stanger had halted a pace or two away, the gun rock-steady in his fingers, and now the second intruder had moved up, and Chick recognized that one also. It was Dugan. The back of Chick's neck began to ache again as he saw the broad, hairy fist that had struck and smashed him into oblivion.

Ott Stanger said, "Take the gun off him, Dugan. He might try to use it."

The big, hair-matted fingers came forward and plucked the weapon from Chick's waistband. Chick Bronson was beyond putting up any resistance; he could only wait with arms raised, head shaking a little as he looked at the well-groomed, sleek figure of the saloon man and the blocky-shouldered giant who out-topped them both by half a head or more.

He said huskily, "The sheriff told me you'd likely want to string my hide for what happened yesterday, but looks like this is going kind of far!"

Ott Stanger's mouth warped into a curious and

unreadable expression. "Listen to him, Dugan!" he grunted to the other man. "Playing dumb. You don't really think I'd give a damn about small stuff like you, just because of yesterday?"

"Well, I dunno what else I ever done to you."

The words were hardly out of his mouth when the saloon man's free hand flipped sharply, across and back; the open palm smacked meatily against Chick's face, jarring him. "As long as you keep talking funny," grunted Stanger, "we'll act rough. Watch your step or I'll have to turn Dugan loose on you!"

Dazed, Chick stood with a fine red thread of blood dribbling down his cheek and stared at the man with the gun. Fury was swamped by an utter lack of understanding and sick dread at thought of big Dugan unloosing the murder in those fists of his.

The stench of scorching meat rose to his nostrils from the forgotten jack roasting over the flickering fire, but he had no thought for that now.

"If you'd just tell me what you want—" he began, half-pleading, and then ducked away wildly as Stanger's six-gun lifted in a threatening gesture. His foot slipped on slick pine needles. He went to one knee, crouched there peering up at his captors.

And Otto Stanger was saying, "You know what we want, all right! The money—the bank loot! We were with the posse that picked up Ward McCarey's trail after the Three Pines job. He lost us for a space of three hours while we went on a false tangent into the hills instead of heading on toward Lost Wolf River, and sometime in those three hours, before we caught up with him in that hay barn at the Lazy F, he managed to get rid of the saddlebags with the loot.

"Fifty thousand dollars! It wasn't in the barn when we took him—he must have buried it someplace. We mean for you to show us where!"

"Me?"

"Quit stalling! The jailer tipped us off that you had words with McCarey this morning before they took him away. He even seen McCarey slip you something. And then, as soon as the sheriff turned you loose, you struck out in this direction as fast as you could travel. The sheriff might be a dope, but to us that all adds. McCarey told you where those saddlebags are buried, knowing he'd never have a chance at them himself. And you're on your way now to dig them up."

"No!" cried Chick Bronson, staggered. "There was never a word said about the money! I swear! I'll show you what it was McCarey give me—just an old, bashed-up silver dollar. Look!"

He was starting to fumble in his pocket as Ott Stanger, with a look of extreme disgust, shrugged and turned away. Stanger jerked his head at the giant. "He's all yours, Dugan!"

Chick came up off the ground, fighting desperately, but he never had a chance. Dugan met him with a hurled rock of a fist that smashed into Chick's face and sent him back-pedaling, thrown half around by the blow. He struck the bole of a tree and before he could pull away Dugan was moving in on him.

And then, with cold efficiency, Dugan went to work.

Presently Stanger grunted, "That'll do for now. Don't want him unconscious. I'll talk to him again." Dugan stepped back, panting a little, and his boss added, "Whatever is making that stink, kick it out of the fire and throw some more wood on—it's dyin' down." Then Ott Stanger moved forward and nudged Chick Bronson with a toe of his shoe. "All right—come to!"

Chick lay face down where Dugan had dropped him. His insides seemed ablaze with pain; Dugan knew where to hit to make his blows count for the maximum of punishment. Chick groaned and lifted his head.

As new fuel added to the fire's effectiveness, Ott Stanger's cruel face came into focus. Chick looked at it through a reddish haze. It was a narrow face, the nose long and sharp, the eyes heavy lidded, the mouth thin and without mercy. It looked to Chick Bronson about the ugliest sight he had ever laid eyes on.

The saloon man said, "You can see now, I hope, that I'm not stringing you; I mean business. And don't think stalling will net you anything—my time's too valuable for that! I intended to follow and watch you dig up the money, but I couldn't wait out here all night while you made camp. Now if you know what's smart you'll stop giving me trouble and do what I tell you."

Chick Bronson, huddled there, shook his head wearily and hopelessly. "I've already said I don't know anything."

"Well, might be you'll change your mind! While

you think it over, we'll be moving on toward Lost Wolf River. We should make it by morning, and I think by that time you'll have decided to use some sense. Dugan"—he turned, yelling orders to his henchman—"bring the horses. And take this guy's sorrel off the picket and throw his saddle on for him. We got distance to cover!"

"Let him saddle his own bronc!" growled the giant. Nonetheless, he did as he was commanded.

Watching dully, with one of his eyes throbbing shut under a punishing blow of Dugan's mauling fist, Chick Bronson wished he'd been told to put the gear on the sorrel himself; there might have been an unguarded moment, however brief, when he could have made an escape in the darkness. But most likely that was the very thing Ott Stanger had in his careful mind. He would not be one to overlook many bets.

Finally, while Stanger kicked dirt over the last embers of the fire, Dugan came out of the timber edge leading a pair of horses. Stanger said harshly: "Up!" And as Chick came slowly to his feet a helping shove sent him lurching toward his saddle. Dugan, already mounted, held the reins. Chick climbed into leather, and a moment later the saloon man had him bracketed on the other side.

"Let's be rolling!"

They hadn't bothered tying him; all too plainly, it wasn't necessary. Exhausted, bruised, and hollow-bellied, Chick Bronson swayed over the saddle-horn and tried futilely to think ahead.

With fifty thousand dollars dangling before their eyes and a firm conviction that they had the means of getting their greedy hands on it, it was plain these two were ready to go to almost any lengths. They wouldn't actually kill him, of course, but they wouldn't stop far short of it; and the fact that Chick didn't have the information they were determined to drag out of him wouldn't save him.

For these captors of his were obviously cruel and without heart, driven only by their money lust and capable of anything. At least this was true of Ott Stanger; the other—big, slow-witted Dugan—was merely a tool who would obey orders and let his boss do his thinking for him.

Now, if ever, was a time to make a man wish desperately for some Samaritan to aid him. And Chick Bronson—a nobody, a drifter in a strange country, utterly friendless—knew he was in this thing alone. Unless . . . Suddenly, with a start, he recalled the silver dollar in his pocket.

Vince Kimbrough, whoever he might be, was somewhere ahead on the Lost Wolf. Chick toyed a bit with the possibility of stalling long enough to discover who Kimbrough was and then using the coin somehow to appeal for help. But next moment his stirring hopes plummeted again as he saw just how unlikely such a chance really was.

So he rode, in deepening despair, through a seemingly endless darkness. His captors said little; there were only the normal night sounds, the jingle of harness trappings, the ragged rhythm of hoof-beats. Ott Stanger set a comfortable gait that a mount could keep up for hours without tiring. But every once in a while he would order a halt to breathe the horses, and in those times, while the three mounts grazed on slipped bits and loosened cinches, he was apt to start bearing down on Chick again.

"Ready to be sensible yet?"

"Let—let me think a minute."

Chick had found by this time that if he continued to protest his ignorance it got him nothing, except to be turned over to Dugan for further treatment with those smashing, hurting fists. He was already torn and bruised and bloody, with one eye nearly shut and the iron tang of blood in his mouth from a cut lip, and his insides so punished that each jolt of the saddle sent pain spearing through him. He sat on the ground now, too exhausted to stand, and squinted up at the shapes of the two who loomed over him, silhouetted against a sky turning pearly with dawn.

Near by the tired horses pulled at high grass. The birds were waking. Ahead, beyond a steep breakoff, the wide and level valley of the Lost Wolf lay sleeping in mists that rose from the broad and looping river, with the rosy light of sunup spreading across the far escarpments. It would have been a beautiful moment, under better circumstances.

The saloon man shifted impatiently. "You've had all night to think. There's the valley, and the loot is down there somewhere. You either make up your mind to talk—right now—or what's happened to you so far will seem mild compared to what you'll get!"

Chick looked at him dully, and at Dugan. In the strengthening light both their faces were tight and strained from the all-night trek, and Stanger's mean regard held a violence that he seemed to be holding back by main effort. In Dugan's heavy features, however, Chick found something else—the beginning of uncertainty. Scowling, the big man shook his head and for the first time voiced a protest.

"I dunno, boss. I've hurt him plenty, and he still won't talk. He's a game little rooster. Much more and I'm apt to kill him, and we still wouldn't know anything."

Stanger shot him a hard look. "What of it? If he don't talk, damned if I care if you do kill him!" He turned back to the prisoner. "Last chance, fellow! Talk, and keep your hide. Otherwise—"

FIVE

Chick Bronson lifted a hand shakily, ran the back of it across his battered mouth. Past the legs of his captors he looked down into Lost Wolf Valley that was glowing now with misty morning colors. His thoughts were forming themselves, taking shape with desperate haste.

He said, stalling for time, "Supposing I show you where the money is, how do I know you won't kill me anyway? That loot belongs to the bank. You'll want to make sure I don't tell on you."

A sour grunt exploded from Ott Stanger. "I'm not afraid of that. You couldn't prove anything, and it would be the surest way of asking for murder. No, you get me the money and I give you my promise to let you go. I'll even let you have a couple hundred dollars out of it for your own poke. Is that fair enough?"

Chick drew a deep breath, let it out.

"I reckon you take the pot," he muttered. "I—I've had about as much as I can stand."

A look of triumph warped Stanger's fatigue-pinched features. "Deciding to be sensible! All right, bucko, tell us where it is."

"I'll have to show you. I ain't too sure, from McCarey's description, but I think I can find the place once I'm in the valley. Besides, I want to be sure I get that two hundred you promised."

Dugan voiced an objection. "But, boss, we can't take him down there in this shape. How would we explain if anyone saw him?"

The saloon man considered this a moment. Then he shrugged. "We can clean him up a little. Wash some of the blood off his face. We're not apt to run into anybody. We'll make it a point not to."

So they went down into the valley, the three of them, on weary and droop-headed horses that took the shelving drop-off trail with legs stiffly braced. The golden banners of sunrise streamed out half across the sky, and the last of the night rose with the river mists out of the long, wide trough.

To Chick's bloodshot gaze it looked like good range

down there—browned by the fierce sunlight of late summer, ready for the first frosts. He made out scattered ranch headquarters that spotted its length, and yonder the crisscross of streets and buildings that would be a town. After that they had come down across the rim and were on the valley's floor, and Chick lost perspective.

"Well?" demanded Stanger, cutting in on his thoughts.

Chick had an answer ready. "I think it's a little to the south of us," he said. "I noticed a sandstone butte that looked like one of the landmarks McCarey spoke of."

"Can't be very much south," Dugan muttered. "It ain't far to the Lazy F, where we picked him up that day."

"Lead out, fellow," Stanger grunted.

They picked up a wagon trail angling off through the bunch grass and followed it. This pointed generally southward but, more important from Chick Bronson's point of view, it skirted the base of a rise just ahead, on which he had already settled for his purposes. He was going to have to try a break, and that immediately. The chances of getting away with his life were slim enough, but he figured he was going to die anyway if he didn't make the attempt.

In maneuvering single file the switchback rim trail his rein ends had been freed and Chick still had them; otherwise there would have been no hope at all of doing the thing he envisioned. He rode silently between his captors, swaying in the saddle—a pathetic, broken figure of a man, but with senses alert and his one good eye keeping a careful check on the two who bracketed his stirrups and on their slow approach to the hill he had in mind.

Then, at just the proper moment, he turned completely limp and, without a sound, went sliding head-first out of the saddle.

He hit the dirt and lay there, eyes closed, bloody face turned up to the blue morning sky. Ott Stanger pulled in his own mount with a startled curse. He looked at the man on the ground, and his thin mouth quirked contemptuously. "Pick him up!" he ordered his henchman.

But for once Dugan refused to obey orders. "*You* pick him up!" the giant retorted. "You're the one wanted him beaten out of shape. It ain't the first time I killed a man with my fists, but something about this kind of makes me sick!"

Down in the dust, Chick Bronson caught his breath and held it as he waited for the outcome. He had hoped it would be this way, but without much confidence. He knew he couldn't handle Dugan. Stanger, on the other hand, was closer to his size. Though in his present state he hadn't many reserves of strength left in him.

There was a moment of quiet, then saddle leather creaked and he knew it was Stanger who had given in. He tensed, gathering himself. A shadow slid across his face. A boot toe prodded him sharply and he gave to it, showing no life as the saloon man, standing over him, snarled: "Come on! Get your pins under you!"

Stanger kicked him again. Afterward, getting no response, the man leaned and grabbed Chick's arm and started pulling him up to a sitting position. His breath was sour against the prisoner's face. All at once Chick Bronson came to life, and he hurled himself against the other, trying for a hold about the waist.

Ott Stanger yelled once and leaped backward, letting go of Bronson, dragging at his holstered gun. Chick struck his hand just as the gun cleared leather and knocked the weapon spinning. He cursed inwardly; he'd hoped to capture it for himself. That being out of the question, he got his grip about Stanger's thighs and hung on, while he tried to maneuver his feet under him.

Still in saddle, Dugan was shouting incoherently. Dust spurted up chokingly about the struggling figures as Stanger fought to break loose. He drove a blow at Chick's head, and the latter felt his grip slackening on his opponent's body. If he lost that hold, he was done for. The knowledge gave him a last desperate spurt of strength. Then he had a boot set into the road ruts and, pushing up, he hurled all his weight against Stanger and whirled him around, slamming his body against the shoulder of Dugan's mount.

Stanger hit heavily, spilling down as the startled animal danced way, out of control for the instant. And in that brief space of time, while Ott Stanger sprawled in the dirt and Dugan was fighting his horse, Chick turned and flung himself at his own tired sorrel.

He caught the saddlehorn and was scrambling for a stirrup as the sorrel took off, spurred by his frantic yell. Somehow Chick Bronson found the ox-brow and with a supreme effort dragged himself into leather. Just as he settled astride, a gunshot broke the morning air.

Looking back, he saw that Dugan had control, and with a revolver smoking in one hand was already spurring after him. Stanger, on his feet by now, was just leaning to recover his lost six-gun. He had it, and ran with it towards his own horse that waited on trailing reins.

Jaw tight, Chick straightened about again to beat his tired sorrel into greater speed with flailing kicks of spurless boot heels. He figured he had perhaps a thirty-foot lead. It would be very thin.

He pulled to the left, circling the rise of land and laying it momentarily between him and his pursuers. Beyond, a gentle slope dropped away in front of him, and at its foot sat the sprawled buildings of a ranch headquarters. He had spotted them from the rim trail and hoped and counted on the chance that they might give him shelter. Right now the chances didn't look too good—there was a long distance yet to cover.

The sorrel spurted over the bunch-grass slope, and now the two pursuers swept into view and came after; they went down that way, strung out, with Dugan's big gelding hard behind Chick, and Stanger a little farther back. And those two were both shooting, their six-guns cracking sharply and bullets making angry, tearing sounds as they ripped past the fugitive. They didn't want to kill him—they were trying to drop the horse, spill him from leather.

The ranch buildings seemed to sweep upward to meet him, getting larger as he neared. This was a small spread—just a house of three or four rooms, a fair-sized bar, and a few sheds—not even a separate bunk shack. A one-man, twenty-cow outfit, apparently, and showing no sign of life just now except for a wisp of wood smoke that curled up from the kitchen chimney. The shooting chase bearing down on it hadn't yet brought anyone out into the open. Probably whoever lived there would be lying low, afraid and hugging cover.

Since the barn was the nearest of the buildings, Chick pointed toward it. He had picked up a little distance in his mad downhill plunge. Now, glancing back, he saw that his pursuers were actually starting to draw rein, convinced, apparently, that he was going to make cover. And this gave him heart.

At that very moment a bullet struck him high in the shoulder. The force of it knocked him spinning out of the saddle.

He lit rolling; sky and earth whirled about him in a dizzy kaleidoscope. But necessity brought him clawing back to his feet, and he saw that the gaping barn door was only yards away. He staggered on toward it, his enemies spurring harder again at sight of him aground and his horse racing off without him.

Lead clipped the edge of the door's closed leaf as,

panting and stumbling, Chick plunged into its shelter. He thought he couldn't have run another step; he lay in loose straw, sobbing for breath, with the fire of his shoulder wound pouring fiercely through him. Still, he wasn't safe yet. The horsemen outside were clattering into the barnyard and it looked as though they would come right in after him.

He raised up, hunting a weapon of any kind. There was nothing handy, only an ax handle leaning against a roof support a few feet away. Chick went scrambling after that, without much hope, and snatched it up.

He climbed to his feet, braced himself with shoulders pressed against the upright and the futile club gripped tightly, as he fought the numb weakness of his hurt. A horseman flashed briefly past the door, raising a film of dust and driving a shot into the darkness of the barn. Chick saw the muzzle flame; smelled cordite as the gun spoke only yards away.

And then, somewhere, a screen door slammed and all at once another gun was sounding: the sharp, flat whine of a carbine. Neither Stanger nor Dugan, he remembered, had had a saddle gun. Whoever this one belonged to was using it hard and fast—firing as quick as he could work the lever and kick out the spent shells. Chick counted four shots, and after that a pause that was filled by the startled shouts of his pursuers. An angry voice cried, "Now, get out of here or I'll put the next one under your hats instead of over them. Go on—scoot! I mean it!"

The bawling voice of Ott Stanger cried, "Don't mix

in this! We want that man in there and we mean to take him."

"I don't see any law badges on you," retorted the one with the rifle. It struck Chick Bronson, suddenly, that the voice belonged to a woman—incredible as that seemed. "And if this is some private feud you can get off Lazy F with it. Whoever that man is, I'm damned if I'll let you have him. He may already be dead!"

Lazy F! It struck a resounding echo in Chick's dulled brain, but at the moment he couldn't place the memory. He discovered that he had lost his club, that he was down on hands and knees in the straw with the dim interior of the barn revolving slowly about him. His shoulder and the whole upper body seemed gripped in fiery pain, and he knew consciousness was slipping from him, even as he realized the desperate plight he was in, the need to stay on his feet and protect himself if that valiant woman couldn't drive his enemies away from him.

He remembered, suddenly, about the Lazy F. According to what Stanger had told him, this must be the ranch where a posse had run Ward McCarey to earth and captured him not many days past. This was the very barn in which McCarey had taken cover, where he must have lain, like Chick himself, hurt and waiting for his enemies to close in on him.

That was as far as he got with his thinking. After that darkness came over him and he knew no more.

SIX

He lay on straw ticking in a wooden box bunk slung with rawhide. It was dark, but as his senses cleared he saw that this was owing to the drawing of a curtain across a window and that the light was strong enough beyond it. He looked around, still dazed. This was a bunk room, simply enough furnished, with three other wood frames, like the one in which he lay, fastened to the walls. None of them were spread with blankets; he was the room's sole occupant. Yonder a door stood slightly ajar, but he couldn't see much through the narrow crack.

Chick pushed into a sitting position, and the lancing of pain through his upper body made him gasp a little. His shirt was gone, and there was tight bandaging across his chest and shoulder on the left side. He felt a bit shaky and yet decided he wasn't hurt badly, because after the first shock of torn and aching muscles he could endure to move all right.

Probably that bullet had only grooved him and done comparatively small damage to the tissues. He had taken as much punishment from big Dugan's fists. Touching his face, he found court plaster on the cuts there. He could see distinctly out of only one eye; the other was nearly closed.

Swinging bare feet over the side of the bunk, he fumbled at the drawn curtain and took a look through the window. He was in the Lazy F house, for out there, past an expanse of barren yard and a well, sat the barn where he had been chased by his enemies. A single horse was in the day corral behind the barn; he saw with pleased surprise that it was his own white-stockinged sorrel which somebody must have caught up and put there for him. From the length of shadows on the distant red-rock rim he figured the hour as late afternoon. That meant he'd slept out the day in this bunk; certainly he'd needed it.

There was a table by the window and on it Chick saw a familiar object—his own battered mouth organ from the pocket of the shirt that his unknown bene-factors had cut away to fix his wound. He picked it up, saw that the reeds were clogged with dirt, and put it to his lips and ran the scale to blow the openings free. He was slapping grit from the instrument against a palm when a footstep in the doorway brought his head up quickly.

"Hullo!" he blurted.

The girl was a real beauty; anyhow, she looked good just then to Chick. She had brown curls and full red lips and a skin that had been tanned darkly by much time spent in the open. There was a stubborn bluntness to her chin that he thought gave her features a certain strength of character. More important, she was smiling at him, her eyes full of friendly concern; and it was a mighty long time since anyone—man or woman—had looked at Chick Bronson with any other expression than what they might have shown an unpopular stray cur.

She said, "I was beginning to wonder if you'd ever wake up, mister. How do you feel?"

Chick told her, uncertainly. "I dunno yet. I seem to be all of one piece, though my left wing is stiffer than hades. Did you do the job of patching me up like this?"

"Grampa did it," she said, and, as though reminded, she turned back to the door and called through it. "Come here, Grampa. He's talking." She added, looking at her guest, "I bet you'd eat something if it was forced on you."

The very mention of food hollowed Chick's insides so that he almost clutched the edge of the cot to support himself. "Golly!" he breathed. "I've lost track of the time since I ate."

"You wait right there!"

She hurried out of the room. Staring after her, he was not too muscle-sore or hungry to be affected by the pleasing shape of her, the unconscious sway of her hips inside a simple but well-fitting house dress. A species of slow astonishment was growing in him, for now he knew beyond any question that he recognized that clear, warm voice of hers. He'd heard it once before, through a haze of pain, as he crouched in the litter of the barn and waited for Dugan and Ott Stanger to come after him and finish him off. This girl, unbelievably enough, had been the one with the carbine— the one who sent them packing. Chick shook his head in utter bewilderment.

A man came into the room, through the doorway the

48

girl had just vacated. He was an old man—incredibly old, and so frail-looking you thought you could break him in two with one hand, but he walked as straight as a ramrod and his white-thatched head held the same stubborn carriage as the girl's. He had a snowy beard that reached to the third button of his shirt. He walked in and sat down on a stiff chair facing the bunk and gave the hurt man a keen, sharp-eyed scrutiny.

He said, "What's your name?"

Chick saw no reason to take offense. With all that these people had done for him, they deserved to ask pointed questions. He answered this one, and continued: "I'm much obliged to you and your granddaughter. It was a bad risk she ran, holding that pair off of me. And afterward, I suppose, you must have had a lot of trouble carrying me here into the house and working me over. That's a lot to do, for someone you never seen before—someone that had all the markings of a first-class saddle tramp."

The old man shrugged. "Never mind that for now. Here's Josie with the grub. Might be an idea if you stopped trying to talk until you'd taken on a little of it."

Grub consisted of a plate of beef stew and biscuits, with wild-cherry jam and watermelon pickles and all the coffee he could drink. Josie brought it to him on a tray, and he wasted no time tying into it. Since breakfast yesterday morning in jail, that was how long he'd been waiting for this.

"Shall we have our talk now?" the old man suggested

as Chick set aside the depleted tray and sank back, stuffed and satisfied. He tossed his guest a sack of makin's to finish off with and hooked bony, blue-veined hands around his knee. "Freedom is our name. I'm Matt. You're in the bunk room of the Lazy F— where our crew sleeps when we can afford to hire one."

Of course Chick Bronson understood the purpose of that comment. The old man was taking care to remind him that times were tough and that it wouldn't do any good to ask here for a job; he knew a grub-line rider when he saw one, and he aimed to begin by being plain discouraging. Chick went on with the cigarette he was building, feeling no particular resentment.

"You don't look so hot, fellow," Matt Freedom remarked as he looked at the other critically. "They must have used a meat grinder on that face of yours. Can you see out of your left eye at all?"

Chick touched the puffed and swollen cheek and winced. "Just barely!"

Josie Freedom had returned from carrying out the tray of dirty dishes, and she stood behind her grandfather's chair, looking at their visitor with sympathy. It seemed to him they deserved an explanation, after the trouble he had cost them, so he told them the story briefly—about Ward McCarey's missing loot, and the saloon owner's unfounded belief that Chick knew its hiding place, and the measures that had been taken to try to force information out of him.

He ended, "This ranch was the only hope I saw of getting away before they finished me. I never meant to put anybody in danger by heading for it. I guess it's the second time in a matter of a week you've had a man hunt staged in your barn!"

Old Freedom nodded, clawing at his beard. "Yes, it was there that McCarey holed up when they run him to earth. That's a sort of coincidence, although our ranch being the first you hit on the rim trail into the valley, I guess it ain't so odd at that—I mean, you both picking our hay barn for a hiding place.

"We didn't either of us happen to be around when McCarey snuck in, but we heard the posse's shootin' from a distance and that brought us in a hurry. They were all over the yard, bayin' like hounds on a warm trail. McCarey had been bad hurt, and at the last I guess he wasn't too careful about burying his sign. They run him down all right, and drug him out, too weak to put up a fight. I got no idea at all what he could have done with the money."

The younger man heard this version of the story with great interest, though it didn't really add a great deal to what he had already pieced together. He rubbed a hand across his scalp.

"Well," he said, "I guess there's no call for me to be sitting here any longer. I've been on your hands long enough, and I feel a hundred per cent better since that grub started working inside me."

The girl said, "It may not be so easy leaving here. You haven't forgotten your two enemies?"

He looked up at her, startled. "Are they still on my tail?" he exclaimed.

"They've been waiting in the brush all day long. I've kept an eye out and caught glimpses of them now and again. Nothing I could use the carbine on —they're too careful for that, of course. But they're out there."

Chick twisted quickly and pawed aside the window curtain for another look at the sea of sage and bunch grass that stretched away beyond the barn and the well in the ranch yard. A wind was rising in the tail end of afternoon, and it tossed the sage clumps so that you couldn't have told whether anyone was hidden there or not, but with a bitter certainty settling within him Chick knew the girl was right.

Ott Stanger wouldn't give up so easily. He hadn't dared rush the house, in the face of the girl's carbine, but he could see to it that his escaped prisoner didn't try to leave. And with nightfall he and Dugan might attempt something more drastic.

After all, there was no one here but a hurt cowhand, an old man, and a girl. Fifty thousand dollars was at stake, according to the saloon man's figuring, and come dark he would make his play. Chick felt sure of this; and he was also certain that he couldn't expose Josie Freedom and her grandfather to any further risk.

Sweating a little, he looked at the two of them. "I gotta get out of here!"

"You haven't a gun," the girl pointed out. "And we've nothing but the carbine. You could take that, but with your hurt shoulder you're probably not strong enough to sit a saddle long!"

"Keep the carbine," he told her quickly. "I wouldn't want to deprive you of your only protection. And don't worry about me—I'll wait until it turns dark and see if I can't figure a way to sneak past that pair. After all, there's only two of them and they can't cover all sides of the ranch."

"And once you get through them?" the old man prompted.

"That depends. There's a gent somewhere in this valley who'll give me help, I think, if I can only manage to reach him. Maybe you folks can tell me where I'd be most apt to find Vince Kimbrough."

He was utterly unprepared for what happened then. It was as though a kind of chill came across the room, like a cloud passing the sun; its shadow touched the faces of the Freedoms and, watching, Chick saw them stiffen. He saw Josie's firm brown hands tighten on the back of her grandfather's chair.

Josie answered him, the words bursting from her and tense with some unnamed feeling. "Is Kimbrough a friend of yours? Is that—?"

The old man broke in quickly, one blue-veined hand lifted to silence her. He sounded stiff and formal and, somehow, tired as he answered Chick Bronson's question.

"It ain't hard to find Vince Kimbrough. Generally town is the place he hangs out. Got an office there. Anybody can direct you—if you're sure you want to find him?"

Abruptly he stood up, and there was a finality about

his whole manner now. "I reckon we've talked as much as will do us any good. You look like you need more rest. Josie and I will keep watch on that pair in the brush, and when dusk comes you can leave."

He looked at the girl. She nodded and slipped out of the room, not meeting again Chick Bronson's stunned glance. A moment later the old man followed, his back stiff and his white-thatched head held high. The door closed behind them, and Chick was left alone with his bemused and puzzled thoughts.

As quick as that—with the bare mention of Vince Kimbrough's name—the atmosphere had changed, and these people lost all their friendly interest in him. Sitting there on the edge of the bunk, he could only shake his head and wonder.

The grub-line trail he followed had certainly got twisted and complicated in these few hours since he slipped Ward McCarey's lucky dollar into his jeans. . . .

SEVEN

Old Matt Freedom was at least right about one thing— despite the rest he'd had, Chick was still weak from the shock of his hurt shoulder and the weight of food in his stomach made him groggy. He stretched out again and presently even slept a little, fretfully, but even then his mind was busy and his thoughts were feverish, grotesque.

He woke to a lurid, reddish light that filled the room and, sitting up, peered through the window. He saw that sunset was on the world. The dying of day had brought a sheet of tumbled cloud across the sky. Against the western horizon the sun lay heavily, a swollen drop of blood behind that broken lay of tattered gray. Shadows were already spreading through the wind-whipped stretch of sage beyond the ranch yard.

Chick Bronson rose and prepared to attempt an escape from the Lazy F.

In the kitchen, which opened off the bunk room, Josie Freedom had a lamp lighted and was working with pots and pans, preparing supper. The shades were drawn, and Matt prowled from one window to another, peering out into the windy growing darkness. The old man didn't even look at Chick Bronson; the girl had little enough to say to him.

At his request she poured out a basin of hot water and, using Matt's razor, Chick worked carefully at his tender face, scraping off as much of his beard as he could manage, though when he was through it looked patchy enough, with its squares of court plaster and blotched, livid bruises. Josie had brought him a shirt, too, that belonged to her grandfather. Taking it, Chick tried to thank her, but she turned away without answering.

His jaw set hard. These people had clearly lost all their liking for him and were now being no more than coldly civil. He felt that they were in a hurry for him to be gone and leave them alone, and he made up his mind that he would oblige them just as quickly as he could manage.

He put on the new shirt, replacing the bloody ruin they'd had to cut off him in tending to his wound. He felt in his jeans pocket to make sure the lucky dollar that would be his introduction and token of assistance from Vince Kimbrough was still there. He checked on his other few belongings, then, taking his shapeless Stetson from a chair back, he returned to the kitchen.

Josie Freedom stood by the big range, looking at him with a kind of sullen animosity. "I've got coffee ready," she said in a dull voice.

He shook his head. He'd taken enough from these people. "No, thanks. I reckon I'll be going now. Any sign of them?" he asked, turning to old Matt.

Freedom, at a window, shook his grizzled head without turning. "They're still somewhere around. They keep circling the place. But it's so dark outside now I've lost 'em."

The girl said, "I went out a little while ago and tied your sorrel to the corral gate. I thought it would be easier for you to saddle him that way."

He showed his appreciation for her clear thinking. "Why, that's fine," said Chick, and going to the door lifted the latch; with his hand on it, he looked at the girl and nodded to the lamp burning yellowly on the center table.

"If you'll douse the light just for a minute, until I can get the door open and shut again . . ."

A minute later he was on the roofed-over stoop, with the door closed between him and the warm security of the kitchen. Shoulders against the rough clapboards of the house siding, he felt the wind pull at him, heard it rattle a loose shingle overhead and sough among the eaves, and an uneasy jumpiness began kicking in his belly.

Somewhere in the windy darkness two men were waiting, listening for sound of him. And remembering Ott Stanger's gun and the man-breaking fists of big Dugan, the sweat came out upon his face and the palms of his hands. He didn't want to leave his shelter. He didn't want to walk out there to meet that danger a second time. But he had it to do.

He wiped his slick palms across his jeans as he probed the darkness with eyes that were gradually accustoming themselves to it after the lamp glow of the kitchen. Not that there was much that anyone could see in a night so devoid of any gleam of starlight. Mainly by guesswork he fixed the location of the corral and started for it, stepping high and feeling his way with the greatest caution.

It didn't help any to know that the corral was one place they would most surely be watching for him.

His outstretched hand found one of the rough wooden bars and he trailed along it, hunting the gate. An iron-shod hoof stomped the dust. He murmured anxiously, "Easy, horse!" He found the end of the rope where Josie had tied it. He slipped between the bars, and at his sorrel's side patted the twitching flank a time or two, saying, "Let's be quiet about this!"

Blanket and saddle were racked across the top pole near the gate, the bridle hooked to the horn. Chick located them and got them on the sorrel, working by feel. When everything was ready he unhooked the gate and swung it open. It gave forth a long-drawn, dismal creaking sound that turned him cold with horror.

Frozen motionless, he waited to see what would happen, but nothing did. Maybe the noise hadn't been so loud as it had seemed to overwrought nerves; or maybe it had failed to carry any distance above the whipping of the wind. After a moment of this agonized waiting he decided there was nothing to do but move ahead.

He took the bridle and walked forward through the gate, leading the sorrel.

The ground slanted away a little in front of him; at the very bottom of the slope, he knew, the brush began. He had decided that if he got that far without stirring trouble, he would then mount and take his chances in flight. But crossing this open space— maybe moving straight toward a waiting gun—the less target he could make by staying on the ground the better he figured his chances. And so he went ahead like that at a cautious prowl, searching every sound in the windy darkness for the presence of his enemies.

It seemed to him that time had halted. The blackness distorted distances. After a few rods he couldn't say how far he had traveled or how much ground lay between him and the dubious haven of the brush. He did know that he had left the hard-packed surface of the ranch yard behind him and that bunch grass brushed his boot tops now. Once he glanced back toward the house and saw the dim square of the shade-drawn kitchen window, and it was so far above and behind him that he was surprised to see how much ground he must actually have covered.

Moments later his sorrel's iron shoe struck some wooden object and booted it away with a startling clatter. And somewhere within yards of him the voice of big Dugan exclaimed: "Hey! What's that?"

Chick Bronson dropped at once to his haunches, horrified at the thought that he had almost stumbled into the big man. He crouched like that, listening, and after an endless, trembling moment Dugan's voice came again, in a hoarse whisper, "Boss! That you, boss?"

A fiery constriction in his chest told Chick Bronson that he was holding onto his breath, and he let it out, slowly. His hand, groping to balance himself, touched something hard then. It was a length of wood, his fumbling fingers told him—a spoke from an old wagon wheel. This must have been what the sorrel's shoe had struck to betray him. Hardly even thinking, he picked the thing up and tested its balance.

The feel of the crude, heavy club put a thrill of reborn confidence in him, poor a weapon as it was; at least it was a weapon, and until that moment he'd had nothing. Silently he shifted the reins to his left hand, cradled the splintered length of wood in his right; silently he came up onto the balls of his feet, hefting it.

Once more—louder, this time—big Dugan called: "Boss?" And, getting no answer, fired.

He had misplaced the origin of the sound he'd heard, so that his shot was far off. The stab of muzzle flash showed him standing with big legs widespread, body crouched above the gun, his horse a black shape behind him. He was perhaps a dozen yards away.

Chick drove himself forward with a long plunge of cramped leg muscles, letting the club fly at arm's length in a wide, flailing swing. If the first blow failed, he knew there would be small chance of getting in a second one. But it didn't fail. He felt the impact as it struck home against solid bone. A sound of pain broke from big Dugan's lips.

Then Chick was swept off his own feet by the carry through of the swing, losing the club completely. Hastily he scrambled forward, and found himself pawing at Dugan's crumpled body. The big man was motionless—not dead, but knocked out by the blow.

He sank back, shaky from the closeness of the thing, his wounded arm hurting. Still, there wasn't time to relax, for Ott Stanger would have heard that shot.

Chick stirred himself and began hunting the weapon Dugan had dropped when he fell. He couldn't find it, though he groped for it in widening circles over the black ground. The blow of the club must have sent it spinning.

He slapped the other's pockets in the faint hope of finding a second gun, but there was none. And now, above the whipping of wind in the brush close by, the thud of hoofs sounded, drawing quickly nearer.

Frantic, and giving up the search, he scrambled to his feet. The sorrel had spooked a few yards, but he groped his way to him and caught the reins before he could move farther away. He got the stirrup, shoved his toe in, and swung up. That other rider was quite close now.

An inspiration drove Chick forward, jumping his sorrel into the brush beyond Ed Dugan's prone shape. Dimly he saw the man's horse, and he rode straight at it, whipping off his battered Stetson. With a yell he brought the hat down on its rump, and that was all the scared pony needed to send it off at a hard gallop, cutting straight through the thick brush.

Ott Stanger heard the crashing, and he let out a bawl of excitement. "Ed! Ed, where are you? Damn it, he's getting away? Stop him!"

Reining in to hold his sorrel quiet, Chick waited. Then he heard the sounds of Stanger's bronc veer sharply, take off in the wake of the galloping horse. As he listened to crashing sounds both animals made shouldering through the dry brush, a grin split the pinched, taut-muscled planes of his face.

"I'd thought he was too smart a fish to rise to that bait!" he grunted.

At best, it was only a minute or two that the trick had gained him; the loose-running horse would likely soon get its trailing reins hooked up and Stanger would learn what he had gone chasing after, and then he'd be back. Quickly Chick pulled his sorrel around and gave him a kick. He started away from there at a

61

good pace, cutting a wide angle from the direction the other horses had taken.

The lights of the Lazy F, at the base of the slope, dwindled behind him and finally dropped from sight as the brush-choked bunch grass hills intervened. After that he was all alone, with the scudding clouds overhead the stiff, chill wind slapping against him. At intervals he reined in and keened that wind for horse sound, hearing nothing but the noises of the night.

Still, he couldn't feel safe. After each pause he kept pushing ahead some more, riding blind in these unknown, chopped-up valley bottomlands. His only impulse was to put so much distance between himself and that other pair, from whom lucky circumstance had freed him, as to earn some measure of confidence that he wouldn't fall into their hands again.

At last some of his panic settled and he pulled rein to let his tired horse take a blow. Even so he found himself starting for a quick look around him at every unexpected noise in the gusty darkness. The third time this happened he hauled himself up, figuratively speaking, by the nape of the neck.

"Come on!" he told himself scornfully. "Catch holt of yourself! You've lost them; after the clubbing you gave that Dugan gent it's not likely he's even come to yet. So forget 'em both! The main thing now is to try and find a way into town. It's no night to spend in the open—not with the rain that's blowing in behind that wind!"

An occasional warning drop had already lashed at him, cold and stinging against his face and the backs of his hands. Chick Bronson shook out the leathers. Going by instinct, he pushed ahead, using every rise of land as a vantage point from which to search the darkness ahead for light which should mark the buildings of Lost Wolf.

EIGHT

He found the town, eventually, but the storm found him first. It hit with a fury of wind-driven icy arrows, and added the final discomfort to Chick Bronson's bruised and bullet-torn soreness. Caught without a slicker, he hunched soddenly in the saddle, quickly chilled to the bone. His hurt arm ached. He was wondering if he would ever be comfortable again when, quite unexpectedly, the trackless course he was following took him across the shoulder of a juniper-clad ridge, and through the gnarled and dripping branches he caught his first glimpse of the town lights scattered below.

A grunt of lifted hope broke from his chilled body, and he gave the sorrel a kick. Minutes later, having maneuvered the tricky descent of the slope he dropped at last into a level wagon road angling across the ridge, and this took him finally into the head of the main street itself.

It was nothing more than a cow-country center, like a hundred Chick had seen during these last disheartening months of hunting a job. It lay on a bank of the river, a huddle of buildings along a crisscross of wide streets, the latter turning muddy now and the rain making long, glancing spears of brightness wherever it crossed a lighted window. But it looked wonderful to Chick Bronson after all he'd gone through reaching this place.

Nevertheless, he knew his first qualm of misgiving. He had nothing, after all, but that battered silver dollar in his pocket and McCarey's vague promise that it would stand him in good stead with this unknown Vince Kimbrough. It seemed suddenly foolish to have banked so heavily on such slim assets, but he possessed no others.

The streets were almost deserted. Chick stopped a lone figure that went slogging past him and, leaning from saddle, asked, "Where would I find a man named Kimbrough?"

This question earned him a curious look. "Tried his office?"

"No. Where is it?"

"Middle of the next block. If you don't find him there, you might ask at the Bull's Head—he owns that too."

Chick said thanks and rode on, searching now for something that looked like an office. He found the place at last. It was a small, box-shaped structure with a sign that was dimly visible through the rain: KIM-BROUGH LAND AND CATTLE COMPANY. The windows were dark, however. A little farther on, and across the road, a saloon made a splash of light and noise; he decided that might be the Bull's Head and angled toward it.

It turned out that it was—a big, two-storied frame structure standing with its back to the silent flow of the river. Chick Bronson put his sorrel among the few other broncs that stood hump-shouldered, tails into the storm, and swung down to wrap stiff rein leathers about the soggy pole. He reached into a pocket, fumbled out the battered silver dollar.

"Well, better wish me luck, pony!" he grunted. "What happens now determines whether you get anything to eat and a warm stall tonight!"

He clumped across the walk and up the three steps to the double glass doors.

The Bull's Head was not very lively. A pair of men stood at the bar, talking quietly over their drinks. Four or five more were clustered around a card table, near the big iron stove that had a fire crackling in it against the chill of the rainy evening. A mechanical piano jangled but no one appeared to be listening.

A few heads had lifted as the door opened, but after a curious glance at the bedraggled stranger they turned away. Chick pulled off his soggy hat, beat it against his leg to knock some of the wet out of it, and dragged it on again. Then, dribbling a trail of water from his dripping clothes, he walked over to the bar.

The bartender was a mean-eyed individual, and something in his chill regard put Chick in mind of the welcome he'd got last time, in Ott Stanger's place. He

65

swallowed and gave the man a nod that he tried to make pleasant and at the same time businesslike.

"Is Mr. Kimbrough around?"

Slowly the barkeep's fishy stare traveled the length of this stranger's shabby figure. The thick lip curled. "No handouts, bud!"

Chick felt the flush begin to creep up into his battered features. "This isn't a handout," he retorted. "I want to see him about a—a business matter."

"Likely!" snorted the bartender. But now one of the other pair of men standing at the bar interrupted before Chick had to make an answer.

"It's all right, Joe. I'll talk to him."

Chick turned quickly, guessing that this was Vince Kimbrough himself. He saw a tall and gaunt figure, with heavy brows and a prominent nose and dugout cheeks and a long, clean-shaven jaw. His hair was thick, graying at the temples. His eyes were gray, too, and brooding, his deep voice mild. Vince Kimbrough gave you the impression of great reserve; no man was apt to know very clearly what went on behind his high and bony forehead. Had he worn a beard, Chick thought he would have looked considerably like Abraham Lincoln.

He said pleasantly, "Just what was it you wanted?"

"Why"—Chick Bronson took in a long breath, decided on his approach—"to buy you a drink, Mr. Kimbrough." And he placed Ward McCarey's battered lucky dollar on the shiny mahogany between them.

Vince Kimbrough's bushy brows drew into a frown.

66

He looked at Chick and at the coin. And then he picked the dollar up, turned it over in his long and tapered fingers. The bar lamps glinted light from the spot where a bullet had pitted the silver.

The gray eyes lifted, speared Chick Bronson's. "This belongs to Ward McCarey, and McCarey is in jail. What are you doing with it?"

In the fewest possible words Chick told him the story. Kimbrough heard him out with that brooding expression settling deeper about his mouth and the gaunted lines of his hollow cheeks. He shook his head as the other finished.

"Too bad—too bad!" he said darkly. "I'm sorry about Ward. He was a good man, but foolish in his way. Like so many others, he thought he could stay ahead of the game. He couldn't see that, going on that way, knocking off one bank after another, he was bound to have a poor ending.

"I wish there was something that could have been done, but once he let himself get caught—and with a murder charge on his head—it was too late. They'll hang him now, while other men, and worse ones, will get rich and die in bed of old age because they had just a little more brains!"

Then, throwing off this mood with a shrug, Kimbrough turned his attention once more to the man beside him. "So you're looking for a job," he said, and his voice and his smile were suddenly friendly. "Well, if McCarey promised with practically his last breath that I would help you, I certainly don't see how I can

67

let him down! But in the meantime, what about that face of yours? And your hurt arm? Looks to me the first thing you need is to see a doctor!"

"It's all right. The people out at the Lazy F were real kind to me, and fixed me up. They did a good job."

He thought Kimbrough's glance deepened a little. "Lazy F? That's the Freedoms, I guess you mean." He didn't pursue the subject, but asked instead, "Where did you get so bad beat up? In that jail?"

Briefly Chick explained what had really happened. And Vince Kimbrough's expressive face turned thunderous under the heavy brows.

"I know Ott Stanger!" he grunted. "And if he understands what's good for him he'll keep his small-town crookedness away from this valley! I won't put up with him!"

"That gorilla of his, Ed Dugan, is pretty dangerous," Chick observed.

"Bob Creel, here, is dangerous himself!" Vince Kimbrough nodded toward the man with whom he had been drinking at the bar.

Creel was a slight man, no bigger than Chick, and with a wrinkled, sun-darkened visage whose age was hard to determine. If he was dangerous, Chick decided, it would have to be in a different way from the bruising muscular power of the brute Dugan. And then, looking into the man's cold, slate-blue eyes and at the gun strapped down against his slabby thigh, Chick thought he could guess where the danger lay.

"They'd better not think they're going to get away

with anything here," Kimbrough was saying. "Right, Bob?"

Unsmiling, the gunman nodded. There seemed to be a complete understanding between these two, and Chick began to wonder a little if Bob Creel might be on the other's payroll. It hardly seemed possible that so quiet-spoken and seemingly sincere a man as Vince Kimbrough should feel the need of a bodyguard. But then he remembered, in a flash, the way the Freedoms had acted at mention of Kimbrough's name, and it created in him a moment's confusion.

Still, he supposed, that was how it would always be. Let a man rise in the world and there were always others bound to resent and hate him for it.

Now Vince Kimbrough shoved back toward Chick the battered lucky dollar, and to the man behind the bar he said, "Give him his drink, Joe. On me." He reached into the inside pocket of his sack coat, drew out a long leather wallet and removed a couple of bills from it, placed them on the bar in front of the stranger. They were twenties, Chick saw, and his eyes boggled slightly.

"This should do you for tonight," said Kimbrough. "Get a place to sleep and a meal under your belt. I still think, too, you had better see that doctor. Tell him I sent you."

Chick swallowed, but did not touch the money. "I meant just what I said, Mr. Kimbrough. I didn't come here for a handout. "It's a job I want—a chance to earn my way—"

His benefactor cut him off with a smile and the wave of a hand. "Of course," he said. "I understand that. Believe me if I didn't think you were worth helping I wouldn't do it, even to please Ward McCarey's ghost.

"There's something about you I like, Bronson, and I can usually find ways to use a good man. You look me up tomorrow morning, and we'll see what we can work up in the nature of a job."

Chick Bronson nodded. "Yes sir," he said lamely, his gratitude past forming itself in words. "I—I want you to know I—"

But another smiling shake of the head dismissed his attempt at thanks. Vince Kimbrough walked away a moment later to watch the card players, and Chick Bronson picked up the two twenty-dollar bills, feeling their crispness with fingers that trembled a little at his good fortune as he folded them, stowed them away in a pocket of his rain-soaked jeans. A shot glass of whisky had been placed before him, and he nodded to the bartender, lifted the drink, and downed it slowly.

Ward McCarey's silver dollar still lay before him. He took it up, turned it over between his fingers, and tossed it thoughtfully on his palm. For Chick Bronson, at least, it was indeed proving itself a lucky charm!

NINE

With the drink warm inside him he left the Bull's Head, a considerably lighter-hearted man than the friendless derelict who had entered a few minutes earlier. Money in his pocket and the promise of a job—however indefinite the nature of it still remained—these were enough to open an entire new world, and his good fortune in meeting Vince Kimbrough had Chick almost unconscious of the driving, needling rain which had so tormented him before.

His first concern was for the sorrel, waiting miserable and droop-headed at the hitching rack outside. After the patient animal had been taken care of would be time enough to think about his own belly—empty again, the generous grub he'd eaten at the Freedoms' having worn itself out—and a hotel and a warm, dry bed. For tomorrow he'd rely on his luck and on Vince Kimbrough's promise.

He untied the sorrel, climbed into the wet saddle, and went through the rain looking for a public stable. A lantern swaying above the wide doors and wooden ramp led him to one a block from the river.

As Chick rode into the musty interior a man in horsy-smelling overalls came out of the cubbyhole office at the front of the barn. Giving a suspicious look to the stranger's outfit, he muttered something about payment in advance; but his expression changed when

Bronson dug out one of the twenties and offered it to him.

"Hell's bells, mister!" the night barnman grunted. "I ain't got no change for that kind of money. Pay me when you leave."

He started to take the sorrel, but Chick said, "I'll look after him myself. Just tell me where to put him."

"Any stall that's empty." The man clumped back into his room, and Chick busied himself with unsaddling.

The bridle leathers and the latigo were stiff to his numbed fingers, the blanket soggy and heavy with soaked-up moisture. He got them hung up, and pailed out oats from the bin, and gave the sorrel's gaunt barrel and legs a quick rubdown. "There," he said, that finished. "Maybe now you'll feel less like you belong to a no-good tramp!"

He tossed aside the gunny sack he'd used, straightened, and reached for his coat that he'd thrown across the stall partition while he worked. Shrugging into it, he walked out of the stall, leaving his starved horse muzzling busily at the grain. He saw Ott Stanger and big Ed Dugan in the straw-littered runway, waiting for him.

Somehow, in the changes of the last half-hour, he had almost lost sight of that pair; had almost forgotten that, even here in town, he wasn't necessarily free of danger. He stopped dead in his tracks, a sick horror rising in him. Motionless and sinister, they stood with the yellow light of a wall lantern gleaming on rain-shiny black slickers, on the six-gun in Ott Stanger's fingers.

"Put the gear back on him!" growled the saloon man. "You're coming with us!"

Chick swallowed without effect at the constriction in his throat. He noticed that big Dugan had a piece of white rag tied about his skull, just visible beneath down-pulled hatbrim, and the rag was stained with blood. The big man saw him staring at it and his lip curled.

"Yeah, you see what you done to me!" growled Dugan, in a voice that was thick with hatred. "You'll pay for it too!"

"First, though," Stanger cut in, "you'll take us to that money. And there'll be no foolishness this time—no tricks! One more phony move, and it'll be the last you ever make. I guess you see by now you aren't going to get away from us!"

Somehow Chick Bronson found his voice. He thought of the man in the barn office, up toward the front of the building, but there was no chance of calling for help. What he said was, "You might as well go ahead and kill me, then. I was only stalling you. I don't know a damned thing about the money!"

His hopes had lifted so high after his talk with Vince Kimbrough that now, finding himself right back in the hands of this pair, his tired spirits took a plummeting drop into despair, and the irony of the thing left him beaten, almost indifferent. They couldn't hurt him much more than they had already, he reasoned dully;

let them get it over with, since it was plain he could not really hope to escape.

"You don't get off so easy," said Dugan. "Not after the trouble you've given us!"

His big hands lifted, the fingers crooking and twisting into fists. He took a step toward Chick Bronson, and the latter only stood and watched him moving in.

Then a voice said into the taut stillness: "Hold it—right where you are, big boy! Stanger, you can drop that gun and step away from it!"

A shock went through the pair of them, visibly. Slowly their heads turned, and past them Chick stared as the gunman, Bob Creel, eased into view around a partition. Creel's weapon was leveled in lean, iron-hard fingers, its muzzle trained straight at Stanger's slicker-clad shape. Creel's slate-blue eyes were narrowed dangerously, his tight mouth quirked in a ferocious, humorless smile.

"Don't make any mistakes," he warned quietly. "Just do like you're told!"

Either they knew Creel by reputation, or they read the warning of peril in his voice and in the catlike grace of his movements. There was no argument. While Ed Dugan stood just as he was, in mid-stride, hands half-raised, his boss let his drawn weapon thump against the straw-littered boards of the aisle. Then at a gesture of Creel's gun barrel he moved back where there would be no temptation to change his mind and try to reach the discarded six-gun.

"Pick it up, Bronson," Bob Creel suggested. "After that, see what kind of artillery the big guy has on him."

Chick obeyed, hurriedly. He breathed a lot easier as soon as he felt the butt of the weapon against his palm. He moved over to Dugan, jerked open the man's slicker, and lifted the gun from the holster strapped about his middle. Dugan evidently had had better luck than he, hunting for it in the brush.

To play safe, he also checked Ott Stanger for a hideout gun but found him clean. He told Creel, "That's it, I guess. They took my gun from me but I don't find it on either of them. I guess they must have thrown it away."

"Why, in that case," grunted the gunman, his smile widening, "I think they should make it good to you. Do you like one of those?"

Chick looked down at the guns he was holding. "Well," he admitted uncertainly, "this silver-handled job I took off Ott Stanger is just the kind of gun I've always wanted to own."

"Keep it, then!"

As Ott Stanger surged forward, bellowing protest, Creel shut him up with a crisp warning. "You ain't running the show now, Stanger! You've beat hell out of this young fellow and you owe him something!" He looked at Chick Bronson. "Go on, kid! Pocket the gun, and while I'm holding them, why don't you go ahead and give these skunks back some of their own medicine? Have yourself a little fun!"

Chick looked at the dark face of Stanger that was missing some of its old arrogance now. He thought with pleasure of a fist smashing against that cruel mouth, flattening that hawkish nose like a ripe tomato, but he shook his head.

"I guess I don't need that kind of revenge," he said, "if they'll just get the heck away from me and let me alone! But I think I will keep the gun!" He added, "I want to thank you, mister, for turning up when you did!"

"Thank Kimbrough! He figured all too likely this pair would have the nerve to trail you clear into town and make a try at you, and he told me to keep my eyes open."

Bob Creel turned to his prisoners. "All right, you've got five minutes. Use them to get out of this town, and don't show yourselves here again. The boss has already told you a time or two that he wouldn't stand for you meddling in his affairs, Stanger!"

"Nobody can run me around!" cried Ott Stanger.

Creel's enigmatic smile only widened. "A big shot back home, but you're not home here in Lost Wolf. And those five minutes are ticking off fast!"

Even though he was in no position to argue, it actually seemed as though the saloon man would defy the ultimatum; but finally he lifted his shoulders in a shrug, and turning away threw a look at his man. "Let's go!" he grunted.

Dugan obeyed, though with pure murder in his ugly face. Under the menace of Bob Creel's gun the two went clumping down the aisle of the stable, wet ponchos swishing. There was a side door by which they'd entered the building. They disappeared through this, and after a moment came the sound of a couple of horses striking off through the stormy night. These sounds quickly faded, and, nodding satisfaction, Bob Creel let his six-gun off cock, shoved it back into a hand-tooled leather holster.

A long breath escaped from Chuck Bronson. His own hand was shaky as he thrust the captured silver-butted six-shooter behind the waistband of his trousers. Looking at the other man, he said, "Things happen too fast for me! I hope you and Mr. Kimbrough don't have any trouble because of—"

"Forget it!" said Creel. "This ain't the first time we've tangled with Ott Stanger. He'd like nothin' better than to spread over onto this range, only he never will as long as Vince Kimbrough is around to keep him out!"

He laid a friendly hand on Chick Bronson's shoulder. "Don't you worry about a thing, kid. I can tell when the boss likes a man, and I don't mind saying he's taken a liking to you. You're in!"

"Well, that—that's fine!" said Chick. "Swell! Only—" He blurted out a thing that was troubling him. "Do you suppose Mr. Kimbrough could think the way Stanger does—that I'm holding out about that fifty thousand? That I really do know where Ward McCarey hid it? I swear I'm telling the truth!"

"Listen, kid! The one thing Vince Kimbrough ain't

got any use for is a liar. If he didn't think you were playing square with him—right across the board—he wouldn't have another thing to do with you. That answer your question?"

Chick Bronson nodded. "I reckon."

"All right. Shove a good meal under your belt, maybe let the doc look you over, and then get some sleep. Come morning, things will look a lot different to you."

"They look different already," Chick admitted. "Just to know I won't be ridin' the grub-line."

TEN

He slept long and hard, and when he finally levered himself out of a bed at the hotel it was to find that he felt at least a hundred per cent better. The bullet-hurt shoulder was still stiff and needed favoring, but his face, as reflected in the streaked mirror nail-hung above the washstand, had lost a good deal of its swelling, and much of the battered soreness had left his body. His breakfast appetite was enormous.

Filling his lungs at the window, he looked out over the muddy streets and houses of the little town, over the shining river that poured rain-swollen beneath the plank bridge and curled in a band of molten sunlight across the rolling valley bottoms. Last night's storm had blown itself out, but today would be cooler because of it—full of wind, and sun, and scudding cloud shadow. He hoped it would prove a good day for him.

Determined to make a presentable appearance when he reported to Vince Kimbrough at the latter's office, Chick located a barbershop as soon as he had eaten and ordered the clippers run through his shaggy mop of hair. Afterwards, at a dry-goods emporium, he proceeded to equip himself with a new outfit to replace his worn-out duds.

This took much of the forty dollars Kimbrough had advanced him, but he felt now that he looked at least halfway human, in new denim jacket and jeans, with copper rivets shining as though polished, and a red-checkered shirt and blue cotton neckerchief. He hadn't been able to promote a new hat, but he'd picked up a pair of secondhand boots that were better than the ones he had been wearing. The tag of a Bull Durham sack dangled from his shirt pocket, and the gun he had taken off Ott Stanger was stowed away in a pocket of the jumper.

When he walked into the land company office it was to find Vince Kimbrough ready to leave and giving a few last-minute instructions to an elderly clerk who sat writing at a desk stacked high with account books and important-looking papers. A wide-brimmed, high-crowned black hat accented the leanness of Kimbrough's dugout cheeks as he nodded greeting.

"Their figure is too high," he said, finishing his business with the clerk. "Tell them to come down three cents on the pound and I might deal. As it is, there's plenty of cattle, in better condition than that Arrowhead stock, that's beginning for a buyer, and

I'm holding more now than I've got grass to feed."

Turning to Chick, then, and buttoning a dark alpaca coat across his gaunt frame, he said, "I'm just riding out to see about some property—looks as though I'd make a deal this morning, so I'm afraid I won't be able to talk to you now." He glanced over the new clothes. "You're some improved. That must have taken quite a chunk of the money I advanced you; do you need any more?" He started to reach for his wallet.

Chick Bronson assured him quickly, "There's a little of it left. I don't want to take any more from you until that job is settled and I can be sure I'm going to be able to earn it."

The other nodded approval. "Stick around then, and if I close this deal for the Barnes property there'll be a job for you all right. On second thought," he added, "maybe you better come along. I might need you to witness the signing of some papers. Get your horse, will you? And join me here as quick as possible."

"Sure thing, Mr. Kimbrough."

Returning from the livery, he found his new boss mounted on a sleek, deep-barreled palomino that showed money and breeding in every line. Bob Creel was there as well, and the three of them rode out of town along the river road under the busy, windy sky.

"By the way, young fellow," Kimbrough remarked suddenly. "I wonder if you heard the news about your friend McCarey?"

Something in the somberness of the man's tone

80

made Chick swing a startled look at him. "What news?"

"A rider came in this morning who'd just been through that country, and he told us. McCarey tried to make a break while the sheriff's escort was taking him back to Three Pines. They killed him."

"Killed?" Chick echoed the word, and then speech choked off in him. Bob Creel put his comment into the stunned silence.

"That must have been near as bad as hanging—to go out with a bullet in the lung. Funny thing too. It took him right through the pocket of his shirt, where he always used to carry that lucky dollar piece—"

"Shut up, Bob!" exclaimed Kimbrough sharply.

But the damage had been done, and Chick Bronson could feel the color draining from his face. He thought, in horror, That damned silver coin! If Ward McCarey hadn't given it away—

"Don't think about it," Kimbrough advised him, in quiet sympathy and understanding of his unvoiced thoughts. "How can we know about these things? It might not have made any difference; with so many guns against him, one or another was bound to tag him out. And I know he'd rather have taken it quick than to hang."

For a long time no one spoke after that as they went ahead at an easy, reaching gait across the bunch-grass swells. But despite anything that could have been said, the silver dollar in Chick Bronson's pocket was like a heavy weight, dragging upon his conscience. . . .

It soon became evident to Chick that all the grass they saw this side of the river was the common graze of certain small-tally outfits similar to the Lazy F, while he gathered that Vince Kimbrough, through his land and cattle operations, controlled most of the range westward of the Lost Wolf to the cedar benches and timbered foothills beyond. The Barnes place was one of these smaller spreads, apparently, about on a par with the Freedom ranch but not so well kept up.

The few buildings, of log and tar-paper construction, sat among a scatter of pines near a murmuring creek. The corrals were small and inadequate, and a rusty pile of empty tins had grown in the yard, within easy throwing distance of the window beneath the stovepipe chimney. Chick guessed from the look of things that Homer Barnes was a solitary—a bachelor. If there had been a woman hereabouts she surely would have made some impress upon the slovenly look of the ranch.

Barnes himself, when he came slouching to the door of the house to greet his visitors, seemed a man wholly fitted to his surroundings—loose-strung, lantern-jawed, with a shiftless, beaten air about him. Seeing who his callers were, he showed his teeth in a weak grin, and scratching with blunt fingers at a scraggly yellow beard, said, "Hello, Mr. Kimbrough. I kind of thought it would be you."

"You said you'd have your answer by this morning," the latter replied. "You wanted twenty-four hours to think it over."

"Uh-huh, I know."

The man showed signs of acute discomfort, while the three of them remained as they were, not dismounting but waiting for an invitation. Finally Barnes ended an awkward silence by turning into the house with a shrug of rounded shoulders. "Reckon you might as well come inside," he told them. "We can discuss the thing some more."

Kimbrough swung down, and the others followed suit. But when Chick started to trail across the yard, his boss halted him. "It looks from here," Kimbrough said, frowning with impatience, "as though he isn't ready to close—not without a little more talk, anyway. Maybe you'd better stay outside until I call you, and keep anyone from disturbing us. This might take some time."

"Whatever you say." As the others moved inside Chick found himself a seat on the stoop's edge, before the door, where he could keep an eye on the horses and also have a clear view of the trail.

The drone of voices came from within the house, but Kimbrough's business dealings held no particular interest for him; Homer Barnes, he gathered, had been offered a price for his buildings and range stock but he was being slow to make up his mind about accepting. While they talked turkey, Chick lounged and idly watched the flow of sun and shadow over the slick green needles of the pines, where the winds made their humming.

Presently he fetched out the harmonica from his

shirt and began to blow on it softly. He found that his thoughts had reverted once more to the terrible news he had learned, of Ward McCarey's death. This depressed him badly, and in such a mood the strains he drew from the old mouth organ were his most soothing medicine.

He was interrupted by a thud of approaching horses in the trail. Knocking spittle out of the mouth organ, he slipped it back into his pocket and leaned to spit out the brassy taste that the battered instrument always left in his mouth. A pair of riders came into sight; Chick was already on his feet before they pulled in their horses, and for a moment they stayed in saddle giving back his stare of surprise.

One was a man, a good-looking chap of thirty or thereabouts—a rancher, from the plain sign of him. The other was Josie Freedom.

It was the girl who spoke first. "Why, what in the world! I never thought we'd be apt to see you again—not after we heard the shooting last night. Grampa and I didn't see how you could have got through it!"

"I done all right," said Chick. "I made it in to town, and after that there wasn't no more trouble."

She said, "I'm—I'm glad. We were worried."

The man with her said, scowling darkly, "Then this is him, Josie? The saddle tramp you said was looking to hitch up with Vince Kimbrough? Looks like he got what he was after, then!" He pointed toward the knot of ground-tied horses. "There's Kimbrough's palomino!"

A sound of distress and disappointment broke from the girl's lips. "Kimbrough's here ahead of us! And we're too late!"

"Maybe!" The cowman's bronzed features had settled into hard lines. "We'll see!" With that he started to lift his right boot from stirrup, to swing down from leather.

Chick Bronson remembered instructions. He had taken a spread-legged stance before the door of the house, and he swallowed once and said, "I'm sorry. You can't go in."

The other held his movement, settled slowly back into leather. His attention was narrowed now on Bronson, and his eyes had clouded. "We can't do what?"

"I work for Vince Kimbrough," Chick Bronson said. "The boss told me not to let nobody disturb them."

"Is that a fact, now?" Scorn dripped in the other's too-quiet voice, showed in the glance he let range over the whole length of the one who had set himself to block the door.

"Well, if that's the way it is, you punk saddle tramp, let's see how you're gonna go about stopping us!"

ELEVEN

"Martin! Don't!"

The girl's cry was an involuntary outburst. Paying no heed, her companion already had one gloved hand on the butt of his belt gun, starting to lift it out of holster. Chick Bronson, for his part, had not looked for anything like this and he was caught staring, startled past thinking of the gun in his own jumper pocket.

"Go ahead!" the man in the saddle challenged him. "Keep us out if you think you can! We know what's afoot inside that house, and we're here to stop it!"

"Why, in that case, Talbot," said a quiet voice, "just step right on in!"

Chick Bronson looked around quickly. Bob Creel had moved into the door behind him and stood there with the point of one shoulder leaning against its edge, his slim right hand dangling loosely and not even touching the gun handle that jutted from his upshot right hip. And yet, Chick thought, the advantage of a half-drawn gun was suddenly as nothing, and the quick shooting of fear into Martin Talbot's brown face showed that he knew the danger he was in.

The one in the door smiled slyly. "Why, what's the matter, hombre? Aren't you coming in, now you been invited?"

"Damn you, Creel—" Talbot's bitter voice broke off futilely. With a savage gesture he shoved his own weapon deep into leather and lifted his hand to the saddle horn where it lay tight-clenched, white-knuckled.

At this Creel chuckled a little, and then he spoke to Chick with a jerk of his head toward the interior of the shack. "Boss wants you, kid," he said. "He's ready for you to witness a couple of signatures."

"All right."

Creel drew aside to give him room, and it was with distinct relief that Chick Bronson welcomed the chance to make a quick escape. He didn't know what was going on here. He knew only that this unexpected and not understood threat of near-violence had knotted his insides for him and parched his throat.

The shabby house contained one small room. As Chick entered, Kimbrough turned from a window through which he must have been watching the goings on outside. Yonder, behind a crude deal table, Homer Barnes sat with hunched shoulders, looking at the papers spread before him and at the steel-nib pen and ink bottle that lay ready for his stubby fingers.

"Well, Barnes?" said Kimbrough, prodding him.

But now there was a sudden flurry of running footsteps, and despite the gunman stationed in the doorway Josie Freedom came bursting into the room. Shoving past Chick, she went directly to the table. She leaned both small fists on the edge of it and she cried, "No! You can't do it! You can't give in to him!"

"I dunno why I shouldn't be able to sell my own property," mumbled Barnes, "when I get a good price for it. Better than sitting back and waiting for the bottom to fall out of the market entirely and leave me with nothin'!" But he didn't look at her as he spoke, only at the fingers that fumbled nervously with the bill of sale in front of him.

She said, "You can't, because it isn't fair to the other members of the Pool—and because it's against the agreements we've made!"

"Agreements?" Vince Kimbrough came striding over from the window then, and his mobile features appeared really troubled. "What's this, Barnes? I've been doing business with you in all good faith; am I to understand that you're tied by commitments I hadn't heard about?"

"Oh, you've heard about them, I think!" Josie retorted, flashing a look at him. "You knew that every member of the Pool had promised not to transfer his property and grazing rights without permission of the others. And you knew just why that arrangement was made!"

The man who sat at the table squirmed uncomfortably. "There wasn't nothing on paper," he protested doggedly. "Honest, Kimbrough, they've got no strings on me or my property."

"Are there no strings on your honor?" Josie Freedom demanded. "Doesn't a promise mean anything?" She impulsively reached to seize his arm.

But her touch seemed only to stir him to resolution. With a quick, angry gesture he shrugged her hand away and then, snatching up the pen, he stabbed it into the ink and in a hasty scrawl slapped his name across the paper. When he threw down the pen, his narrow chest was lifting to his tight breathing.

"There!" he cried hoarsely. "It's done! Go ahead, call me what you like, but I've taken a beating in this damn country, and the way things are going, another six months would have finished me. I tell you there's nothing left to fight for!"

"No, nothing!" cried Josie Freedom, answering him; her voice was choked and trembling, and Chick saw that tears glinted in her eyes. "Nothing—except all we've been building for, here on the Lost Wolf: our homes, our stake in the future . . ."

Martin Talbot spoke up. He had followed as far as the doorway, halting there with the dangerous presence of Creel to check him from daring to cross the threshold. He said, "You're talking to a deaf man, Josie! You can't expect Homer Barnes to understand about the things the rest of us wanted. A man without family or friends, who turned the very house he lived in into a pigsty— he was the weak link in our Pool from the beginning. We might have known he'd be the one, finally, to sell us out and set the wolves loose among us!"

"Now just one moment!"

A hint of color had touched Vince Kimbrough's face, yet his voice was still held down, his anger controlled. "I wish you'd tell me why you people hate me so bitterly!" he said. "Trading in land and cattle is my business; I make a fair bargain, and I keep it. Barnes here will tell you that the price I'm offering him is a good one—better, in fact, than it needed to have been, considering the state of the market."

Talbot's mouth twisted. "Oh yes. I can imagine! It was well worth your while to name a figure he couldn't afford to turn down—one to make him swallow his principles and forget what he owed the rest of us. You figure you've got to get a toehold, at any price, here on the Pool's side of the river. You've gone and overloaded your own graze, clear back into the cedar benches and the foothills, but you need still more room to put the cattle you've been buying up, at panic prices, from better men than you who have been ruined by the slump.

"Now, holding Barnes' membership and his share in our grazing rights, you mean to start pouring your cheap beef onto Pool graze, and you won't stop until you've crowded the rest of us off. And when someday the market starts back up and beef is worth something again, there you'll stand—alone—the biggest damn cattle baron in the state!"

For a moment there was silence—a silence that seemed overpowering after the sound of Talbot's raging voice. And slowly, in that waiting moment, a subtle change came over Vince Kimbrough.

The spare body of the man drew taller, stiff with anger, the deep-set eyes veiled in darkness, and the jaw muscles bunched visibly beneath his sunk-in cheeks. "Bronson!" he snapped. "I called you in here to get your name on that paper—as witness to Barnes' signature!"

Forgotten during the interchange, Chick was brought up with a start to hear his own name hurled into the quiet of the room. But without a word he walked forward, picked up the pen, and signed in a blunt, angular scrawl. As he laid the pen down, his eyes met Josie Freedom's for an instant. There was no warmth in them, nothing beneath their surface—only a frigid hostility and hurt.

He turned away, and Vince Kimbrough said, "All right. Your turn, Bob."

The gunman came into the cabin at an easy slouch, shouldering Talbot aside. When he had affixed his signature, Kimbrough took the paper, scanned it briefly. Then, from the inside pocket of his coat, the latter brought out a narrow length of paper and tossed it down in front of Homer Barnes.

"There's my certified check, in full," he said. "As we agreed, you have a week to wind up your affairs and turn over this property."

He looked at Martin Talbot and the girl. "I wish you could believe that I don't want trouble—with anyone; but apparently you insist on your own wrong notions. Yes, it's true I've been buying up a great deal of cattle, and buying it cheap. I admit I hope to make a profit before the thing is finished. Still, at the same time, let me remind you that I've also saved a lot of ranchers from losing everything they owned and at least left them a stake with which they can hope to begin over again later.

"As for you Pool ranchers, I can only say that you have no reason to be afraid of me. I assure you no one is going to be crowded out. There's room for all of us here on the Lost Wolf!"

"Sure there's room!" snarled Talbot. "If the rest of us are willing to lie down and let you walk all over us! But we won't do that! We'll fight you—you slick-talking, pious devil! And we'll fight this sale! It was made contrary to agreement and it won't stick!"

"I think it will," the other replied quietly. "Take it into court and I think you'll find that any alleged, verbal agreement will carry little weight against a signed bill of sale."

"Probably so, in your court, before your hand-picked county judge! But there must be other ways of fighting, and we'll find them!"

Bob Creel muttered, "I know one way, and I'm inviting you to try it right now, mister. If you feel lucky!"

"Shut up!" Vince Kimbrough silenced his man with a stern look. "If they insist on a war, they're going to have to start it; I'm hoping they will see their mistake. At the moment there apparently isn't anything to gain by talking, so we might as well end this before worse things are said!"

He picked his hat from the back of a chair, made a formal bow to Josie Freedom, nodded to Homer Barnes. Then, without another word, he turned and unhurriedly walked from the room.

Bob Creel slouched out after his boss, but Chick Bronson hesitated a moment. He saw Josie Freedom take the check that Kimbrough had laid on the table, look at it coldly and then at Homer Barnes; her face was tight and miserable, her voice shook a little.

"There it is," she said. "Take it."

The man put tongue to lips, shuttling his glance between her and Martin Talbot. But he didn't move to touch the check, and Josie laid it down again on the edge of the table. Talbot grunted, "Aw, let's get out of here and leave this Judas alone!"

He took her elbow. Josie still looked at Barnes a moment; she shook her head and told him quietly, "I'm so very sorry for you!"

They were gone then, and Chick slowly followed outside. Kimbrough and Creel were already in saddle, waiting for him; as Chick walked over to his sorrel and got the stirrup, he watched Talbot and the girl mount and go riding off along the trail, holding their horses close together in earnest talk.

Something must have shown itself in his face, for when he lifted and settled into leather he saw Vince Kimbrough's frowning look centered on him.

"Well, young man," said Kimbrough quietly, "you heard it all. Maybe you felt what they said was true, and in that case you'd rather not go to work for me. I won't hold you. You can keep the money I advanced, and we'll call it settled—as a sort of tribute to Ward McCarey."

And indeed for just one moment Chick Bronson hesitated over his answer. He couldn't doubt the sincerity in the charges made by Talbot and the girl, or their very real fear of Kimbrough's intentions. On the other hand, he found it mighty hard to meet this man's level gaze and believe anything wicked or dishonest of him.

He cleared his throat, his decision made. "I reckon," he said, "if it's all right, I'd like to stay awhile."

"Fine! Fine, Bronson!" Kimbrough picked up the reins. "We'll count it settled, then."

TWELVE

Stretched out full length upon the sagging bed in his hotel room, Chick Bronson had a chance now to sort out the events of these last crowded days and find his way among them.

The lucky silver dollar was in his hand and he studied it, turning it over and over, thinking of its history and the curious set of events that had brought it to his possession. He thought of Ward McCarey—dead now, they told him; of Ott Stanger and his bodyguard. What had become of those two? he wondered uneasily. Surely they didn't intend surrendering what they saw as their chance at fifty thousand dollars just because Bob Creel had driven them off the night before? No, they would be somewhere around, still waiting, still biding their time.

And then there was the girl. Josie Freedom. . . . The image of that brown-haired girl came and for a moment crowded out all other thoughts: she had made that deep an impression on him. Which of course was only natural, considering that Chick Bronson was a young man, with a young man's normal interests. True, the mere needs of self-preservation had long forced such thoughts into the background. It was only to be expected that they would return, now that his prospects and circumstances had so suddenly improved—and especially with such a particularly handsome young woman to call them forth.

The disturbing thing was the way her whole manner toward him had changed, and all because of prejudice against the man for whom he worked. She had behaved nicer when he was a jobless, hopeless drifter; now that Chick had a job, and presumably was in a position to hold his head up, the coolness she had shown at Barnes's place was highly irritating.

Slowly a resolve took form inside him, and all at once he swung his legs off the bed, reaching for his denim jacket hanging on a chair near by. From its pocket he drew the fancy silver-mounted gun that he had taken off Ott Stanger and thoughtfully tested the weight of it; broke the weapon and looked at the loads.

He was no gunman, but even in his hands this did a lot to level off the odds supposing Stanger was still hanging around waiting for a chance at him. At any rate, he was bound he would not go on hiding in a corner. He would take a little ride this evening—out to Lazy F, where he could try for another talk with Josie and her grandfather, to clarify the situation that had risen between them. If he just kept his eyes open, he ought to be able to take care of himself despite danger of that pair from Hondo Forks.

The decision made, he quickly set to work getting ready. Wind-pushed clouds were already touched with the fires of sunset beyond the window at his elbow. He broke out the new razor he'd bought and, standing before the wash table and the cracked mirror on the wall, had his second shave that day. It was a ticklish job, because of the bruised and cut condition of his face.

He was about half-finished when a knock sounded.

He sang out, and Vince Kimbrough entered the dingy hotel room.

At the brooding look on his employer's face Chick quickly laid down the razor, saying, "Is there trouble, Mr. Kimbrough?"

"It may be," Kimbrough agreed, in his deep voice. "I hope not. Go ahead with what you're doing. I'll just sit here and we can talk."

He let himself down onto the edge of the sagging bed. He appeared very tired, with a worried cast to his eyes, yet his first remark was for Chick Bronson's feelings and for the shoulder whose bandage he had revealed in laying aside his shirt.

Flexing his arm, Chick said briefly, "It's coming fine, Mr. Kimbrough. Hardly stiff at all."

"Good!" And then the man added, turning abruptly to the concern that was apparently large in his thoughts, "I've got something I'd like to have you do for me, if you will. Tonight."

"Why, sure." After all, he could wait to pay his call on the Freedoms. "Whatever you say, boss."

"I'm going to take a chance on you, Chick. You've got a capable look, and I have an idea you would be loyal to a man you worked for. Now that I've bought the Barnes place, I'll be needing someone on the spot to manage it for me. What would you think of that job?"

Chick Bronson was a little flabbergasted. "Why— why, it would be great!"

"Well, I'm considering it. Those Pool ranchers

might be more apt to accept you than they would one of my regular crewmen from the Box K. Their suspicions of me could hardly extend to a young fellow who's new to this country and on the very face of it no crook—no tough gunman.

"Anyway, I'm going ahead with plans to buy that Arrowhead stock, since I can make a good price and will have grass now to put it on. My range boss, Spud Lantry, is getting a wagon-and-trail crew ready to bring them to the Lost Wolf. You'll ride with Spud—it's a job that will take a couple of weeks. And afterward, assuming you stack up and show him you have cow savvy; we'll decide for certain about trying you in the manager's job. That agreeable?"

"Plenty!" the younger man added, "But what was it about tonight?"

"A kind of ticklish assignment, I'm afraid, yet I'll have to ask it. I've learned, indirectly, that because of what happened this morning some of the leaders have called a gathering of the Pool at Martin Talbot's place. It could be considerable of a session, and I'd like very much to know how it develops."

Chick Bronson frowned uncertainly. "You want I should try and crash it?"

"Why, according to my interpretation, buying out Homer Barnes makes me a member of the Pool myself and gives me every right to send a representative to any meeting involving my interests. Of course," Kimbrough admitted, "the others might not see it that way. I said it was ticklish."

"It's that all right!" Chick took a turn over the drab, worn carpet. "Will the whole Pool be there—the Freedoms and everybody?"

"The Freedoms in particular."

Well, he had already decided he would pay a call on Lazy F that night. Attending this meeting at Talbot's would fit in with his own plans. "Sure, I'll go," he said. "Maybe they'll throw me out but they'll have a tussle doing it."

"Don't start trouble," Kimbrough warned him quickly. "If that's what I wanted I'd send Bob Creel. You going, instead, ought to help them see our aims are peaceful. I want to cooperate with the Pool. Try to make them understand that."

"I'll do what I can," Chick promised.

The meeting was already in progress when he rode in out of the windy night, watching the lights of Talbot's small place and thinking with some uneasiness of the reception he was likely to get. He found a good deal of bustle here, with saddle horses and buggies and ranch wagons waiting in the yard and a stir of activity visible through the windows. Martin Talbot's two-roomed bachelor headquarters was filled to overflowing.

There were a dozen small ranchers in the Pool, and from the size of the crowd these must all have brought their families and their crews, such as had them. Dismounting and tying his sorrel to a buggy wheel's spokes, Chick Bronson listened to the hum of voices.

He hitched up his belt, walked across the muddy yard, mounted the three slab steps to the porch. Hand already lifted to knock, he hesitated for the briefest instant, then put his knuckles firmly to the wood and at once heard talk sheer off.

Footsteps approached the door; the latch was lifted and when it swung open it brought him face to face with Martin Talbot himself.

Chick thought at first the man had failed to recognize him, but perhaps it was only unexpectedness that kept him staring blankly for an instant. Then Talbot's face stiffened. He shot a quick glance past the newcomer, to see if there were others. Finding no one else, his eyes came back to Bronson's face, and there was coldness in them, and a sharp wariness in his first challenging words.

"What do you think you want?"

"Vince Kimbrough sent me," Chick answered briefly. "I'm to represent him at this meeting."

Someone echoed, "*Kimbrough?* Now I guess we've heard everythin'!"

"Get out!" Talbot made a move to slam the door, but Chick had other ideas. He put his shoulder against the panel and slid past into the room.

He had a first impression of many sun-darkened faces and hostile eyes, of voices lifting confusedly. There were women here as well as men; he looked for Josie Freedom and found her, half-risen from her chair, one hand clutching at the arm of her frail old grandfather. Her look was one of utter consternation.

Talbot pulled Chick Bronson's eyes back to him now saying hotly, "This is just about the size of something Vince Kimbrough would do. He can't break up the Pool, so he sends a spy!"

Already Chick could see his peaceful mission falling flat; still, he had to make his try at talking reason into prejudiced ears.

"Mr. Kimbrough has a right to be heard and ask the rest of you for co-operation. He wants nothin' but what's good for the valley. And me, I don't take kindly to being called a spy—for any man."

"Then you can best get out of here and stop acting like one! We've put up with enough from you for one day, Bronson."

But suddenly Chick had ceased listening. His busy glance, scanning the faces that filled that small, modestly furnished room, had sighted the pair who stood against the back wall where the potbellied space heater had at first partly hidden them. His head jerked as though to a physical blow.

"*You!*" he blurted.

Ott Stanger returned his look with a tight grin that held unplumbed depths of malice. "This guy giving you trouble, Talbot?" the man said. "Don't worry! Me and Dugan would be mighty pleased to take him off your hands!"

THIRTEEN

Stunned, Chick Bronson could do no more than stare during the space of time that it takes to count three slowly. When he found speech, it was to demand hoarsely, "Who let this pair in?"

"We're here on invite!" snarled Dugan. "We're throwin' in with these good people, and we know just what should be done with a Kimbrough spy!" His big hands lifted suggestively, the thick fingers spread as though they would reach across the room and fasten on the intruder.

Chick whirled to face Martin Talbot. "I can't believe it! You surely wouldn't tie up with two such as these?" But the answer was there, in Talbot's stern, bronzed face; it was reflected in all the others, as his eye ran swiftly across them. In desperation Bronson turned to Josie Freedom and her grandfather.

"You drove them off your place with a rifle yesterday," he pointed out. "Are you forgetting that so quick?"

"I've explained all about yesterday," Ott Stanger cut in harshly. "I've told these folks what a cheap crook you are—how we had to jail you in Hondo Forks—and then how you laid for me when you were loose again, to try and hold me up—"

"Why, that's a lie!"

The saloon man shouted him down. "What's more, I've told 'em people outside the Lost Wolf are fed up with Kimbrough running an asylum for small-fry out-laws like you—not to mention the big shots, the men like Ward McCarey. We're tired of you committing your crimes and then sneaking here for safety. And I've promised to throw everything I have behind the Pool in their battle to lick Kimbrough and his army of gunmen."

"Help we're plenty glad to get too!" Martin Talbot said. "It'll cut the odds to a size where we've maybe got a chance!"

"We'll have an army of our own," Stanger promised. "I can get guns aplenty and the men to work them. And there's an earful, Bronson, for you to take back to your boss!"

Lungs swelling, hands knotted hard into fists against his thighs, Chick swung a long stare around the room. Most of the men were standing now, and their dark scowls held no good promise.

Chick Bronson said coldly, "I've heard all I need to! If the Pool is crazy enough to bring in a bunch of mad dogs and set them loose on this range, then it's plain there's no good to come from talking! I'll tell Kim-brough. And whatever happens will have to rest squarely on your own heads!"

There was the sound of a door being pulled open. "Now get out!" snapped Martin Talbot. "You've had your say. You can leave."

Somebody else muttered, "Yeah—throw him out so we can get on with our business!"

The one man who seemed reluctant for him to go

was big Ed Dugan; Chick saw him scowl, fingering the butt of a six-shooter he had managed to promote somewhere, after losing his own at the town stable the night before. But now Stanger murmured something into his gunman's battered ear, something made Dugan drop his hand away from the gun. Easy to guess what it was. Stanger figured they would have their chance at Bronson later, and without quite so many witnesses.

Chick sought a last look at Josie Freedom and caught her worried frown. Then, with a squeal of boot heel on the linoleum that covered Martin Talbot's floor, he turned and walked out of the house past Talbot's sternly waiting figure.

Outside, he paused long enough to drag on the hat he'd removed on entering; after that he swung down the steps, heading for his sorrel. There was the trample of boots as a couple of Pool men moved out onto the porch to watch him go. They were still there when, finding stirrup, he stepped into the saddle and rode away without a backward look. A rise of excited talk followed him.

He rode a quarter mile or so before reining in to spin a cigarette and consider the meaning of what he had just learned.

Chick had hardly hoped for anything good to come of his mission, but this was far worse than he had dreamed. With Ott Stanger in the picture, stirring up the Pool ranchers and adding his support to their quarrel with Kimbrough, peaceful settlement appeared remote indeed. It would be a fight—and undoubtedly a dirty one.

Stanger's motives were plain enough. There had been trouble and bad blood between him and Kimbrough before, which the humiliation at the hands of Bob Creel last night would not have helped any. Kimbrough had said Stanger would like nothing better than to spread his evil influence over onto this Lost Wolf range. Through the medium of the Pool he probably saw his chance to do just that, and, incidentally, to settle his business with Chick Bronson and the supposed cache of fifty thousand dollars.

While he smoked down the butt, Chick measured this situation from every angle and liked it less and less. As far as he could see there remained but one slim hope, if he was to bring a better report than this back to his employer. There were still the Freedoms. He felt that he knew old Matt and the girl; he felt that they at least wanted to be fair and open-minded.

On a resolution, Chick stubbed out his quirly against battered saddle horn and picked up the reins. He must speak to them—to Josie, anyway. He must try to make her see that all Stanger's talk was a lie. If he could only convince her and her grandfather, they in turn ought to have considerable effect on the others.

He couldn't do it now, of course, with the meeting still in progress. But that could hardly last much longer. He pointed the sorrel toward Lazy F, letting the horse take his own pace.

When he came in sight of the spread and its few

modest buildings, all the windows were dark. The Freedoms hadn't yet returned, and Chick settled to wait for them, first staking out his sorrel at the rear of the barn where there was a patch of graze for him.

Then he hunkered, shoulders against the barn's clapboards, and impatiently smoked down another cigarette while he watched the trail out of the brush, busy churning over that meeting at Talbot's.

He was reaching automatically for tobacco sack and papers when he heard hoof sounds that brought him to his feet stuffing the makings back into his shirt again. Three riders were coming in toward the ranch at an easy gait. Chick watched as they reined in before the house. He heard Martin Talbot say, "I'll take care of the horses, Matt. You two go inside."

"I'll help," Josie Freedom amended quickly. A moment later, to the creak of gear, old Matt was stepping down. While he moved up the steps and into the house, Talbot and the girl came on toward the barn and the night corral, the young man leading Freedom's horse by its reins.

Motionless, Chick Bronson waited. Talbot's presence complicated things, since it was plain enough by this time that there was no use trying to talk to him. And then, having hesitated, Chick knew he had lost his chance to announce himself, for next minute the man and the girl had reached the corral gate, and as they swung down to begin unsaddling they were talking in a way that would have made it difficult to admit he had overheard.

"I suppose you're right," Josie Freedom was saying in a voice that sounded discouraged and tired. "Somehow, Chick Bronson struck me a little different. I thought he was actually what he pretended to be: an honest man that had been hard hit by the slump and couldn't find a job. But the reason he gave for his trouble with Ott Stanger did sound terribly far-fetched; and almost the first thing he wanted to know was how to find Vince Kimbrough."

"Believe me," declared Martin Talbot, as he swung the heavy saddle down from old Matt's bronc, "I know what I'm talking about! There's been lies told, and they haven't been told by Ott Stanger. I've been over to Hondo Forks; I happen to know that Stanger is an important man around there. I certainly would not take any saddle tramp's word in preference to his."

"No, I suppose not."

Standing in the shadows with his back pressed against the barn clapboards, Chick Bronson dug nails into hard palms as he fumed silently. He had to hold back; he was in no position to answer Talbot's accusations. Under his breath he muttered, "Damn stuffed shirt!"

Talbot was still pressing his case against the man he didn't like. "Bronson's just exactly what Stanger called him: another of the petty crooks Vince Kimbrough has on the string to do his dirty work. But we're lucky that he got himself in trouble with Ott Stanger, because it's brought Stanger into this mess on our side, and now we can count on action. Stanger has the power to do just what he says he will!"

"I hope so," said Josie, her voice still tired and without much of the man's enthusiasm.

They went on with their work, and finally both horses were stripped and Talbot choused them inside the pen and swung the pole gate closed behind them. His own mount had been tied to one of the fence posts.

Chick Bronson surmised that, having ridden over with the Freedoms, he meant to stay awhile.

He turned to the girl, taking her arm. "You're worn out. It's been a bad day for all of us."

All at once Josie was crying. "I'm frightened, Martin! What's going to happen to us all? And Grampa—so old, and with trouble like this on his hands. . ."

"Don't worry, honey!" said Talbot soothingly. "Your grandfather's got a lot of fight left in him. Remember, too, whenever you need help, you've always got me."

"I know, Martin!"

They weren't talking now. For a long and excruciating moment Chick heard nothing at all, and he tried to shut his ears to this silence and to look somewhere else than at where the two of them stood, so close together in the darkness. Jealousy he couldn't help rose in him like a powerful flame, consuming all other emotions; but then even this burned away to ashes and left him feeling empty.

After all, why should he allow himself thoughts about a girl like Josie Freedom? Who was he, anyway? A nobody, and on the wrong side in this quarrel. He had no right to be disturbed by the scene which he had, unwittingly, overheard.

"We best go in," Martin Talbot said. "Matt's waiting for us."

A lamp had been lighted within the house by this time, and as the man and the girl moved away from him Chick could see them silhouetted briefly against the square of window glow. They were walking close together, and Martin Talbot had an arm about Josie's shoulders.

Chick Bronson waited until the kitchen door closed. Then, as quietly as possible, he went to where he had left his sorrel; led him for some distance from the ranch buildings before daring to mount and ride unobtrusively away into the night.

FOURTEEN

Trying to be fair, he had to admit that maybe these people couldn't help feeling the way they did about him, having convinced themselves as a premise of Kimbrough's villainy. Even Martin Talbot, though he might be something of a stuffed shirt, was honestly following what looked to him the only course. And there was nothing Chick could do or say to show the Pool their error.

No point, certainly, trying to talk to the Freedoms— not while Talbot was on hand to counter every word he spoke and turn his arguments against him. He had no eloquence, no skill at debate. Likely he'd merely lose his temper, and that would get him nowhere. Accordingly, he turned his sorrel along the town road, to take his waiting boss a discouraging report on the evening's results.

He had covered only a little of the distance when he first became aware that other horsemen were abroad in the night.

Chick pulled up, alarmed and conscious of his own danger. It was utterly black around him save for the dim light of stars obscured by a cloud film. A wind was stirring, rocking brush and tree heads and filling the darkness with deceptive sounds; but, listening and sorting out the other noises, he thought he couldn't have been mistaken. He knew it when, for a fleeting moment, he caught the definite pulse of hoofs hitting a stretch of surface rock, to be instantly lost.

A few rods farther he hauled rein again and this time lifted the silver-handled gun from his pocket. The natural first thought was of Ott Stanger and big Ed Dugan, who had hounded him through wind and storm only the night before. Perhaps they had trailed him from Talbot's place. Well, this time, if they expected to take him prisoner, they would find him with a gun in his hand.

Then a nervous jerk on the reins brought the sorrel pivoting to the right, as a man, running, broke toward him from that direction. One moment there were only the uncertain noises, and suddenly there he was—on foot, a dark figure against the windy shadows. Sight of him startled a challenge out of Chick Bronson, pitched a couple of notes higher than he had intended:

"Hold it! Stop where you are, damn you, or I'll—"

"No! No! Don't shoot!" There was fear in that voice; warping it beyond recognition, yet he thought it had a familiar ring. And he drew confidence himself from the other's evident terror.

"Declare yourself or I will shoot!" he ordered harshly. "Who is this? What are you doing out here in the night without a bronc?"

The man had come to a stand, very near him; Chick Bronson could hear the rasp of panting breath. "You— you ain't one of them?"

"One of who?"

"They're trying to kill me. They caught me on the trail as I was heading home from town. I got away but my bronc threw me and I lost my gun, and they're still after me. And naturally, when I stumbled into you, I thought—"

By this time Chick had placed the faltering, panicky voice. "You're Barnes, aren't you?" Come to think of it, he had not in fact been present at the meeting at Talbot's—which was probably natural enough, under the circumstances. "Who is it that's trying to kill you?"

"I don't know," the other said miserably. "I didn't get to see their faces, and they—But wait a minute! You ain't said who *you* are as yet!" His voice held a quick renewal of suspicion.

Chick Bronson told him, sensing his relief. "No, you

don't have to worry about me. Let me see if I can't help you out of this. I reckon my old sorrel will carry double."

"It could mean dragging you into a gun fight, should we run across any of them."

"Reckon we'll risk that." Bronson added, "How many were there?"

"I—I only saw a couple, but—I dunno. Scared as I was and the racket this damned wind makes . . ."

"No matter. Climb up!"

Chick vacated a stirrup, reaching to pull him behind the saddle. Barnes was rail-thin, without much weight to him, which was just as well if they were going to have to ride double for any length of time.

On his part, Chick had not much taste for this business. It was almost certainly more of Ott Stanger's doings: yet he couldn't, with a clear conscience, desert this terror-stricken fugitive. Duty to Vince Kimbrough, in fact, demanded that he lend Homer Barnes his aid.

So he said, "Which way shall we make it? Maybe you'd rather head back for town where you know you'll be safe."

"It's nearer to the ranch," said Barnes. He had recovered somewhat from his panic and a kind of dogged courage was taking hold. "I got an extra gun at home. Take me there, and I can fort up and look out for myself all right. I'll be damned if I let them run me off! It's my property, until I turn it over to Kimbrough."

"All right. You call the game and I'll try to deal it. The ranch it is, then. Hold on!" He added, "And leave my gun arm alone if we run into trouble!"

He judged they were some five miles from the squalid Barnes place. He set as direct a course as he could, and they moved ahead into the windy night, feeling their way, probing the danger that lurked in every sound and every shifting shadow.

Chick's own uneasiness was helped little by Homer Barnes's harsh breath against his neck and Homer's frightened hands clutching at him. No matter how often he warned the man to leave his gun arm unhampered, he found himself constantly shaking loose of the bony grasp. Half-a-dozen times he had to fight the impulse to empty his gun at a deceptive noise or at some bulking shape which proved to be only a grazing steer that broke and scattered into the darkness as the sorrel stumbled upon it.

Then, abruptly, they had come out of the brush, and the rich, sun-cured graze of the valley bottom spread before them under dim starlight. Chick Bronson took the long rise of a shallow hogback and reined down here to listen and study out the shape of the land that lay ahead. The fantastic contours and disturbing sounds of the brush having been left at their backs, here there was only openness, swept by the night wind but holding no threat.

Encouraged, he said, "Looks quiet enough. Maybe we've lost 'em. Maybe they've given you up."

"Maybe."

At least here in the open there was less chance for an enemy taking them by surprise. They came down off the hogback and rode ahead, pointing toward the river. They passed several bunches of cattle belonging to one or another of the Pool members but raised no sight or sound of a horseman.

Presently the damp breath of the river added its chill to the night, and they could make out the black gash of its channel paralleling their course at a little distance. Somewhat later they entered the fringe of pines and then, in its clearing, the ramshackle Barnes headquarters stood silent and dark.

"Well," said Chick, "you're home."

Barnes grunted something and swung stiffly down. But the way he clung to the stirrup warned Chick that he was still shaken by his recent terror. "Would you come in?" he blurted. "I'd like to—talk."

On the verge of refusing, Chick shrugged and said, instead, "Why not?" He doubted whether there was anything the other really had on his mind. Homer Barnes simply craved company; perhaps he even feared that his enemies, having lost him out in the brush, would come looking for him here and so was trying to hold onto Chick as long as possible.

But though he didn't think he liked Homer Barnes very much, he had been touched to pity by the man's abject fear. He knew what it was to be afraid. "It's early," he agreed. "I guess I can stop for a minute."

As Barnes hurried into the cabin to make a light, Chick dismounted and eased the girths of his saddle.

113

He was reaching for the bridle, to slip the sorrel's bit and let him graze, when movement in the edge of the timber rang its warning.

"No light!" he commanded sharply in a stage whisper that he hoped would reach to the shack. In the same instant he was springing sideward, whirling to face the trees, right hand fumbling for his jacket pocket.

Yonder a gun flashed red fire.

Its report mingled with the shrill neigh of the frightened sorrel. Chick had his own gun out; at a crouch, with the after-image of flame smeared across his vision, he swung the weapon up and cramped trigger. A second shot answered him, and this time the bullet was so close that Chick heard the wild shriek of its passing.

He ducked and stumbled backward, making for the protection of the cabin's gaping doorway. Fortunately Homer Barnes had not yet got a light going to target him, and Chick did not make the mistake of shooting again—not here in the open, with his enemy hidden in the pines and waiting for a muzzle flash. The ambusher felt for him with still another bullet, but this one was wide and stamped into the chinked logs of the cabin.

Then the edge of the stoop struck Chick's groping heel and almost threw him, and, whirling, he made a lunge toward the door and safety. As he went he shouted, "I'm comin' in, Barnes! Don't shoot!"

The thought occurred to him that there hadn't been

any sound from Homer Barnes since the shooting started—not even an outcry. That seemed awfully strange.

"Bronson! *Look out!*"

The shout was muffled, coming from the thick, sweaty-smelling darkness and ending abruptly almost as though choked off. But Homer Barnes's warning had come too late. Chick had already reached the doorsill and he could not stop himself. He lunged across, full tilt, into the man who waited for him there—a man who certainly was not the scrawny Homer Barnes. He whipped up the gun but his hand struck a descending arm and the weapon went spinning.

And then, with the hoarse breathing of his unseen opponent whisky-strong against his face, something that felt like the cabin's very roof came slamming down full upon him. His head, he thought, split like an overripe melon. The earth gave way under him and he fell into nowhere.

FIFTEEN

He was lying belly down, and half-frozen, his face pressed so flat against muddy pine boards that if he could lift his head Chick Bronson figured he would have no more profile than a slab of siding. Only, he didn't think he would ever rouse strength enough to lift anything so heavy as his head felt to him just then. Instead, he twisted it sideward; and even that small movement put a throb of agony through his skull that made him squeeze his eyes tight and clench his teeth while he rode it out.

When this had passed and he opened his eyes again, he found he had to squint against the pale light that lay about him—the indistinct gray filter of dawn in which objects appeared to swim without sure form or outline. It showed him Homer Barnes's cabin, and the place looked a wreck.

The table was on its side, dirty dishes broken and scattered around it. A chair, close beside Chick Bronson, was hardly more than a pile of splinters; he wondered vaguely if that was what they had hit him with. He saw no sign at all of Homer Barnes.

After a while, feeling strong enough, he worked his hands into position with palms against the floor and shoved up. Hell broke loose briefly inside his skull, but by clutching at the jamb of the open door he managed doggedly to pull himself to his feet.

The pain subsided to a persistent, throbbing pulse. Looking around, he saw where his hat had fallen, and he leaned carefully and picked it up. He started to put it on, decided not to just yet.

Then he remembered the gun that had bounced out of his hand last night and he went looking for it, but without success at first. Chick had about decided his attacker must have snagged it when he thought of the space below the rumpled box bunk in a corner of the room. Going down on hands and knees to look there, he found the weapon lying close against the wall. He fished it out, shoved it into his pocket, then, as an afterthought, dug it up and replaced the empty shell. Now, if his sorrel only hadn't been run off in all the confusion. . . .

And again, what about Homer Barnes?

The disappearance was a nagging worry at the back of Chick's aching head. He knew he should lose no time in starting a search. Barnes's enemies, having missed the first try, must have wanted the backsliding Pool rancher pretty badly for them to come and prepare this trap—a stake-out inside the cabin and another at the clearing's edge. Barnes, entering ahead of Chick to make a light, had walked straight into their hands; and that blow on the head had put Chick Bronson out of the way and left them free to work their will. Where had they taken their victim, and what had they done with him?

The level rays of a newly risen sun were gilding the pine trunks now, burnishing their needles with gold. Chick Bronson's sorrel had fortunately not wandered off. He found him grazing, the saddle slipped on loosened girths to hang upside down beneath his belly. It looked as though the sorrel had tried to rid himself of this burden and, failing, had decided to make the best of it.

Chick drew on his battered Stetson gingerly, then walked over to the bronc and got the heavy saddle yanked around where it belonged and the cinches drawn tight. Afterward he led the horse back to the cabin, his frowning attention on the ground where he might hope to find evidence as to what had become of the missing rancher.

It was a search that ended quicker than he ever expected. A morning wind, rising, swept the pine trees and started them swaying. Movement lifted his attention to a stout, low-hanging branch at the edge of the clearing. He froze that way, staring, a tightening of nausea working its way through his empty middle.

Homer Barnes didn't weigh much—scarcely enough to stretch the stiff hemp from which he dangled. In the dappled light and shade of early morning his body swayed lazily, the hard rope creaking. As Chick watched, horrified, the dead man twisted in a slow half circle, until his face came around into view. And that was when Chick had to turn quickly away, sickness knotting up inside him.

He brought the body in with him, tied face down over the back of one of the dead rancher's own horses. He rode slowly along wide streets that were still muddy from the recent rains, pointing straight for Sheriff Mart Murray's office. And though he came without fanfare, there were plenty who saw him pass with the lead animal under its grisly dangling burden. Before he had reached the big square courthouse practically all the town of Lost Wolf knew that something was afoot.

Dismounting, he tied both horses at the courthouse hitchpole. When he came out of the building with Sheriff Murray flanking him, a crowd was already gathering.

Murray, an Irishman with heavy sandy eyebrows and a pinched and humorless mouth, shoved his way through and lifted the dead man's head for a look at him. One look was enough, even for a man hardened by professional acquaintance with violence. He vented a grunt and let Barnes's limp head fall.

"Yeah, it's Barnes, all right. And somebody sure as hell done for him! You're sure you didn't see enough to give us an idea?"

Chick Bronson hesitated. "I didn't actually see anything," he admitted. "It was too dark. One shot at me, and another gave me a wallop that laid me out. There were probably more, but I wouln't want to swear to who or how many."

The sheriff looked at him closely. "You sound as though you had a notion or two though."

"Well, after all, I had heard threats against Homer Barnes. It's well known there were some people mighty put out because he'd sold his ranch and his interest in the Pool."

"That'll be enough" a voice cried loudly, and glancing up Chick saw the rider who had pulled in at the edge of the crowd. He had been at the meeting last night. His face was brick red, and as the crowd in the street turned he threw his challenge at Chick.

"You can keep your damned insinuations to yourself! You aren't going to make the Pool out a bunch of murderers!"

Bronson returned his look coldly, but he felt no urge to make a public brawl. He shrugged and said,

"Keep your shirt on. I don't think I mentioned any names."

"You mentioned the Pool!"

"I didn't say a word that's not common knowledge. Would you deny that you held a meeting last night for the sole purpose of deciding how you could keep Barnes from selling?"

Sheriff Murray cut off a blistering reply the rancher started. "Let's let it drop! You, too, Whitaker! Neither of you better make any more of this until you've had time to think what you're saying!"

And the other held his tongue, though his cheek muscles fluttered with the plain desire to hurl angry speech. He was not looking at the sheriff, however, or at Chick Bronson; his smoldering stare had passed elsewhere and, turning, Chick sighted Bob Creel standing near by, on the edge of the plank sidewalk. The little gunman had said nothing at all, but he had caught Whitaker's eye, and something in the look he gave the Pool rancher had the effect Sheriff Murray's order failed to.

Without another word Whitaker jerked his horse away and touched it sharply with the spurs. The animal shied, tossing its head, and he checked it under a firm rein, rode on along the street—a stiff and angry shape in the leather.

Murray told the rest of the crowd, "Break it up now!" And as they began to disperse he turned to Chick. "The coroner will be wanting your story. Likely the hearing can be arranged this afternoon, since there'll be no other witness needed. You'll be ready to testify?"

"Any time," Chick told him, without much interest. "Soon as I see to my bronc and get me something to eat and maybe a stiff drink under my belt."

Bob Creel joined them. "Never mind the sorrel; I'll take care of him. Right now I think Vince Kimbrough will be wanting to talk to you about this business."

"All right."

Vince Kimbrough had heard the news and had his hat on, ready to leave his office for the courthouse. He brought Chick Bronson inside and pulled out a chair for him and put a glass of whisky in his hand which Chick quickly drained. It hit his empty belly hard but gave him strength that he needed.

"Now, boy," said Kimbrough, his somber face graven with concern, "if you think you're able to talk, I'd like to hear everything you can tell me."

As Chick talked he listened intently, his face growing more and more heavy with concern. "It's damned hard to believe," he said at last, shaking his head solemnly. "To think that those people would be blinded enough, in their hatred of me, to listen to a thug like Ott Stanger, and let him bring the ugliest kind of violence into this country!"

Remembering the Freedoms, and Martin Talbot, who seemed decent enough for all he was a stuffed shirt, and a few of the other Pool members, Chick Bronson was forced to say, "I can't honestly believe the Pool had anything to do with it. Whatever their feelings about Barnes, they wouldn't be capable of condoning such things."

"I hope not. If you're right, could be this will wake them up—shock them into cutting loose from Stanger before it's too late."

"Or maybe," Chick suggested darkly, "it's already too late. Maybe there'll be none with courage enough, for fear they'll get the same treatment! It's obvious Barnes was murdered as an example to anyone else who might dare to think for himself. Stanger's losing no time! He's got a foothold now, and unless something can be done to stop him he'll have these river bottoms running in blood before he's through!"

Vince Kimbrough leaned and touched the other's shoulder. "Don't let yourself worry about it," he said. "Believe me, this country isn't gone completely to the dogs. Stanger will be stopped, and in good time. You can take my promise on that!"

SIXTEEN

The coroner's jury brought in a finding of "death at the hands of parties unknown," and within half an hour the inquest was over. This could have been expected. At Vince Kimbrough's suggestion, Chick in telling his story had stuck close to the facts of the killing itself, not mentioning anything that happened earlier. Since he could not identify either man who shot at him or the one who clubbed him unconscious in the dark doorway of the shack, there was small use in speculation.

Nevertheless, the Pool membership had evidently feared the inquest would take a different turn. Long before hearing time they were already pouring into town, sober-looking riders who left their horses tied along the hitch racks and gathered in silent knots on street corners and under arcade roofs, waiting for things to start. Chick Bronson, from his hotel window, had watched this with considerable uneasiness. And then, only minutes before he would have to descend the stairs, a sudden thunder of hoofs striking the resounding planks of the river bridge heralded other new arrivals.

It was Box K, with Bob Creel at their head! They rode in without hurry, spreading out as they hit the end of the main street. Sunlight struck bright glints from spurs and belt buckles, from the polished metal of saddle guns, the brass cartridges in well-filled shell belts. They looked neither to right nor left, not returning the angry scowls directed toward them as the Pool men saw their numerical superiority reduced to nothing.

And it was into this atmosphere of tense expectancy that Chick Bronson emerged, to begin his uneasy passage to the courthouse.

Now the brief and perfunctory ceremony was over. Verdict had been pronounced by the tobacco-chewing jury foreman. An audible sigh of relief ran through the courtroom, and then a stampede had started for the doors.

Bob Creel and Vince Kimbrough fell in beside Chick as he came out of the smoky room a moment later, glad for a breath of cooler, cleaner air. Kimbrough told him, "There may be trouble even yet. I don't like the look of things out in the street. Some of the Pool men have been liquoring."

"Let 'em start something!" growled the gunman, Bob Creel.

"Yes!" snapped Kimbrough. "Let them start it—we won't! We'll say or do nothing unless we're forced to. Is that understood?"

They came out of the dark center hallway into the sunlight. From the top of the broad steps Chick Bronson looked over this scene and measured its danger.

There were saddle horses and ranch teams tied all along the street. Directly across from them a few Pool men who had hurried out with the first word of the verdict centered a rapidly gathering crowd of their friends. Bronson saw Whitaker, Martin Talbot, other leaders. As they caught sight of the three on the courthouse steps, the group broke apart as at a signal, spreading out and turning.

For a long moment then no one stirred anywhere. A big maple that lifted its autumn branches into the sunlight dropped a few crimson leaves upon the silent Pool men, to sift down to earth unnoticed. That was the only movement.

Said Bob Creel, out of the side of his mouth, "I ain't seen anything of Ott Stanger."

124

"You won't, either," Vince Kimbrough answered positively. "He hasn't the guts to show his face. He's hoping these dupes of his will tangle with us. He wouldn't care how many got killed, if they just rid him of us."

"They'll start nothin': a bunch of yellow bellies!"

"They're peaceable men," Kimbrough corrected him. "The hands will fight, all right, if the owners tell them, but the owners are mostly family men. And that will hold them back—unless feelings have got too strong. Let's go!"

Deliberately, unhurriedly, they dropped down toward the muddy sidewalk plankings.

Then from the top of the steps behind them the voice of Sheriff Murray sounded—pitched loud, so that it carried well along the silent thoroughfare. "Well, Mr. Kimbrough," he said, and the three stopped and turned back. "That was a fair inquest that nobody can object to. Now it's my job to locate the skunks who murdered Homer Barnes, and I'll be counting on every man here to give me the help I need doing it!"

Somewhere a voice called scornfully, "Hired tin badge!"

The sheriff's Irish face turned crimson. He swung his head in a quick, searching look but failed to spot his heckler. He straightened out the fingers that had knotted into fists alongside his legs.

"You'd think it was Saturday," he muttered finally, "the number of people there are loafing around town with nothing to do. Seems to me it's high time this foolishness stopped and people got back to work, else I might have to start clearing the town of vagrants!"

Vince Kimbrough said without rancor, "You can't blame folks for being concerned. What happened to Homer Barnes was just about the most shocking thing this county's ever seen, and I don't think there's any man that wouldn't do anything possible to run down his murderers. Isn't that right, Talbot?"

He got no answer. There was no break in the taut stillness; and it seemed to Chick Bronson, right then, that anything could happen. The high tension that pulsed between these two opposing groups could spark violence, set loose the fury of guns. . . .

A ranch wagon turned into sight at the corner of the street, came jouncing down the deep ruts. The two people on the seat were Josie Freedom and her grand-father. As the town waited, Josie brought her team to a halt beneath the big maple tree.

Martin Talbot and the others stepped quickly forward. Those across the street could make nothing of the talk as they clustered about the wagon, but it appeared that old Matt Freedom was arguing. And though he met angry opposition, it subsided quickly before the frail old man's eloquence.

"Good!" murmured Kimbrough. "Freedom's talking turkey with them. They'll listen to him. He's a persuasive man. Too bad he figures we have to be on opposite sides of the fence. Come on!" he added. "While he's pouring cold water on them, let's move along and do our bit to help this thing blow over!"

Bob Creel grumbled a little, but Chick was glad enough to see a bad thing come to an end. They went down the street toward Kimbrough's office, not with any haste that might be interpreted to mean that they were running from a showdown. They passed one or two of Kimbrough's riders and stopped as he spoke to a stocky cowhand that Chick knew to be Spud Lantry, range boss for the Box K.

"Get these men out of sight," Kimbrough told him, "but have them stick around in case they're needed. Each hand gets a free drink at the Bull's Head, but no more until we're sure this thing is going to blow over. When you've seen to that, better come over to the office yourself—I want to talk to you."

Lantry said, "Sure, boss," and touched his hat-brim with a rope-calloused finger. But his eyes were on Chick Bronson's face, and Chick read a cold dislike in them.

This bothered him. He had so far never even spoken with Spud Lantry let alone had any trouble with him.

At the land company office Kimbrough poured drinks all around from his private stock. "It could have been a bad business out there," he commented. "Instead of a mere inquest, you would have thought from the way they acted that we had the whole Pool on trial for murder."

"Well, and weren't they?" demanded Bob Creel from the chair where he sat tilted back against the wall, glass in hand. "Does anybody seriously question that it was them hanged Barnes?"

"Why, as a matter of fact, I've heard suggested that it could have been the work of thieves. Barnes brought in my check, yesterday afternoon, to deposit, and some people are saying crooks may have thought he had cashed it, instead, and was carrying the money on him. This is not as clear a case, you see, as you might think."

Chick Bronson put in heavily, "With a pair like Ott Stanger and his bully boy around, it's clear enough for me! No mere thieves would have had to string Barnes up and leave him to—to strangle like that!" Memory of the dead man's distorted features was still powerful enough to stir him profoundly.

Kimbrough sensed his emotions and shoved the bottle of bonded whisky over to him.

"How are you feeling?" he asked, studying Chick closely. "Head bother you any more?"

"Oh no. It's all right." He helped himself to a short drink. "If I can survive the treatment I've had these last few days I reckon nothing can kill me."

"We'll see that you don't have any more trouble like that," Vince Kimbrough promised him.

Spud Lantry came into the office and accepted a drink. Kimbrough started questioning his range boss as to how things were going at the ranch.

The man shrugged. "Quiet as hell. This is the busy season, but none of the outfits are doing any work, since there's no market to ship to. Like the others, we're holding our beef up in the hills on summer range as long as possible; got a crew with them, under

orders not to start moving them down to the botto. until the weather breaks. Don't want to load ou winter graze with beef any sooner than we can help it."

Kimbrough nodded approval. It would seem that Lantry had a free hand in the running of the ranch, his decisions accepted on nearly every matter. "Now, about this Arrowhead stock."

"The wagon's ready and the trail crew picked. We'll be rolling on schedule."

"Good." Kimbrough indicated Chick. "Bronson here will ride with you. I'm putting the Arrowhead beef on that Pool graze I bought from Barnes, and I want him to manage the property for me."

Lantry flicked the new man with a look. "That's a pretty big assignment."

"I think you've heard my reasons."

"But you don't even know him! You don't know that he savvies one end of a cow from another!"

Chick Bronson stiffened. "I've drawn top-hand wages—" he began. Kimbrough silenced him with a lifted hand.

"That's exactly the reason you're to take him with you on the trail—so that you can try and give me a report. It's settled; let's have no argument."

Kimbrough's generally quiet voice had a sharp edge just then, and it was a danger signal that Spud Lantry appeared unwilling to ignore. "O.K.," the range boss said, and drained his drink.

"You'll ride on out to the ranch with the crew

tonight," Vince Kimbrough instructed Chick. "And remember, I'll be wanting to hear a good report from Spud." He held out his hand. "Here's wishing you luck!"

"Thanks." Rising, Chick Bronson shook hands briefly and picked up his hat. At the door Spud was waiting for him. Again he felt the cold weight of the foreman's stare; again it made him uncomfortable.

Only then did he realize exactly what he was up against. He had already undergone a great deal, but it seemed that his testing was not yet finished. To qualify in the job for which Vince Kimbrough intended grooming him, he would have to earn the approval of Spud Lantry—a man who did not like him; a man who was plainly jealous over his abrupt rise to favor with their boss.

Chick gave his jeans a purposeful hitch as he went out through the office doorway.

SEVENTEEN

The trail crew Lantry had chosen consisted of four riders besides himself and Chick and the cook who would handle the grub-and-bedroll wagon. They pulled away at dawn from the big Box K headquarters under the west rim of Lost Wolf Valley. They had a couple hundred miles of trail to cover to the Arrowhead home range which lay in an adjoining state to the south and west; and their trip out, in fine fall weather, and unhampered except for the rattly wagon and the

remount string, ought to have been a pleasure jaunt for strong-bodied, healthy men who reveled in saddle work and the wide outdoors.

But where Chick was concerned, Spud Lantry's manner ruined it.

It could have been apparent from the beginning that the range boss had a bee under his tail. The first hint was the looks on the other trail hands as Lantry assigned Chick his string for the remuda. Even before inspecting them, he knew Spud must have singled out all the most cross-grained, tough-jawed renegades in the Box K horse herd for his use. Nothing would be gained by protesting, though, and Bronson kept his mouth shut. Lantry meant to pour it on him. Very well, he would take it, and turn in a job of work, regardless, which would make it impossible for the jealous range boss to give anything but a good report of him to Vince Kimbrough.

It wasn't going to be easy. Spud was a man of invention, with a fertile imagination for ways to irritate and embarrass someone under his authority. The first camp out, as weary riders stripped gear from their mounts and stretched stiff, cramped muscles, he came over to Chick with special orders which he voiced in a tone unnecessarily loud and unpleasant. "The cook's gonna need firewood, and water from the crick yonder. That'll be your camp job, boy. Get about it!"

Cook's helper. Chick Bronson knew it was meant for an insult. The rest of the crew had stopped whatever they were doing to watch; he saw the grin on the insolent, buck-toothed features of a weedy youngster who called himself the Kansas Kid and who sported a big hogleg revolver on one hip. Chick sensed that the woodhawk's duties generally fell to this half-grown lout and that he was getting a real kick out of seeing them pass instead to someone else.

He merely shrugged. "Where's the ax?" he grunted.

The Arrowhead beef proved to be good, well-tallowed stock in price condition for the market; only this year there was no market, and the harried rancher lacked feed to attempt holding his cattle for a rise. He made a sour face over the size of Vince Kimbrough's certified check, which Lantry handed over in return for the herd papers, but he had no comment.

Kimbrough had got himself a bargain all right, yet his price was better than the owner could have got across the block, and range delivery saved the added cost of shipping.

"It's fair enough," the man said, folding the check and shoving it inside his jeans pocket. "It will buy groceries and keep my creditors off my neck for a spell; maybe even pull me through until another season. Damn it, things can't keep on this way forever!"

"Won't bother me none if they do," Spud Lantry grunted—with unnecessary good humor, Chick Bronson thought. "Well as Kimbrough is doing right now, and the bonuses he pays his crew."

"Not every man is lucky enough to make a cleaning out of times like these."

"Or smart enough," Lantry amended.

At dawn they caught up the herd and started back with it, not pushing the critters, wanting to save as much as possible of the prime flesh they had put on on the home range. Cattle didn't like to quit graze to which they had become accustomed, and the first day of a drive generally found them restless and looking for a chance to turn back—slip past the watchful riders and return to the grass they had left. Knowing this, Chick Bronson was not much surprised when the trail boss singled him out with a stab of his thumb and said, "You ride drag. And keep up them laggers, you hear me? Kimbrough's gonna be expecting a full count!"

Chick nodded shortly, reining away toward the tail of the drive without any useless protest. The dust was bad at drag; tailings kicked up by several hundred cloven hoofs hung in a tawny haze about him. Grit stung a man's eyes and clogged his ears, even working its way between his teeth despite the neckcloth he pulled up.

Even without the sun overhead, it would have been sweaty and miserable enough—a rider's nerves taut from the need of constant vigil as he kept the lumbering steers from turning and bolting past him, breaking for home range.

Chick was glad indeed when they reached the place where the chuck wagon was set up, waiting, and Lantry gave the order to halt. But that did not mean rest, of course. Immediately the crabbed pot wrangler was yelling for wood and water, and there was barely time to strip his tired sorrel before falling to with his camp chores.

Later, riding his lonely stint of nighthawk duty, with only the silent stars and the mass of the sleeping herd for company, Chick Bronson had time to think this business over. After all, he told himself, it would not last but a few days more. He would simply have to outlast Spud's meanness—hold a tight rein, and refuse to give him the provocation the range boss was trying to force from him. If it got a little hard to take—well, even this beat what he had had up to a week ago: empty pockets and no place or job for him anywhere.

Ward McCarey's battered lucky dollar was still working for him. His trouble with the jealous Lantry was simply an inconvenience that he figured he should be able to take in stride.

The second day, the steers had got accustomed to the trail and handled better; also, a wind had risen that cut the rust fog they raised, dissipating and scattering it. This did considerable to ease Chick Bronson's work, helping to lift his spirits.

Come evening, they had the herd settled out on a broad, brushy flat near a clot of scrub timber that edged a mossy seep spring. A dim trail straggled down off a rim, crossing the stream not far from where the chuck wagon was staked out. Chick Bronson, weary and saddle-stiff, had the ax and was in the trees knocking windfall branches into usable lengths for the cook's fire when a lone horsebacker came drifting in along that trail, to pull up and watch the man at work.

Chick paused long enough for a brief nod and a non-committal, "Howdy!"

"What outfit's this?"

He was a gaunt figure, in shabby range garb that didn't look too warm for the season, and there was something desperate in the haunted eyes and fined-down, beard-stubbled face. It wasn't hard to place him—not for Chick Bronson, who a short week ago had himself been just a broken, drifting character as this. When, he answered, the saddle tramp touched tongue nervously to his lips and wanted to know who was the man in charge.

Chick pointed out Spud Lantry, and the other said, "Much obliged, friend," and rode on toward the wagon.

When Chick Bronson walked up from the trees a minute later, carrying an armload of kindling, he saw that the drifter was still waiting a chance to talk to Lantry. He had dismounted and, reins in hand, was hanging back until the trail boss should finish with one of his riders. As soon as the latter had pulled away and was heading toward the herd, the drifter moved diffidently forward.

It wasn't necessary to hear what they said. Chick Bronson had asked for jobs too often himself and been turned down just the way Lantry turned this scarecrow down—curtly, without even waiting to let him finish. A mere jerk of his thumb dismissed the tramp, and Spud walked away leaving him standing there.

The man ran a hand over stubbled jaw and mouth, defeat and indecision in his look. He glanced over at the chuck wagon where the cook was bustling about the drop-leaf gate. Coffee was already steaming over the fire, to which Chick Bronson had just added new fuel; there were biscuits in the Dutch oven, and a stew of beef and potatoes added its aroma to tease a starved man's nostrils.

The tramp sidled over. "How about a bait of grub?" he asked tentatively. "I've missed a couple meals."

With an indifferent shrug the cook pointed to a stack of tin plates and cups and a pile of cheap silverware. Stammering thanks, the tramp got eating equipment and Chick moved aside, making room while he hunkered to ladle stew and biscuits onto his plate.

Spud Lantry turned just then and saw what was going on. Normally no trail boss would object to the cook's putting out free grub for a hungry trail rider if he felt like it. But Lantry was in a sour mood. He glowered at the drifter and at Chick Bronson, who stood a few feet distant. And he vented an angry roar.

"By hell! One saddle tramp bumming chow with this outfit is enough! Didn't I say there was nothing for you here?"

The cook put in quickly, "I told him it was O.K., Spud."

"Well, I'm tellin' him different!" Suddenly, with a quick stride forward, Lantry gave the plate in the man's hand a kick that sent it into the fire, spilling the food there to sputter greasily. As the tramp came scrambling to his feet, Lantry growled, "Now, beat it!" And he turned his back.

For a moment the other stood as though stunned, the empty plate and wasted food lying in the ashes at his feet, his face white behind its beard stubble. Then a sound that was like a sob of rage broke from his twisted lips; one hand stabbed into his jacket pocket, and as it emerged the drifter was lunging after Lantry.

Chick Bronson saw the streak of the metal blade lifted. There was no time to call a warning. Hardly thinking, he started forward, overtaking him only a step behind the unsuspecting trail boss. He caught the upraised arm, gave it a yank. Pulled half-around, the tramp lost balance and spilled heavily. And Chick hurled himself upon him.

He felt the quick bite of steel slice across the back of a hand as he groped to capture the knife blade—missed. The man under him struggled and twisted, bearded face contorted, lips pulled back from gritted teeth. Still, he had little strength in his starved and stringy body. Without much trouble Chick got his arm pinned to the ground beneath one knee, found the wrist, and twisted sharply.

A grunt of pain broke from the other; his fingers opened, letting the knife go, and after that the tramp went limp completely. He lay panting as Chick Bronson picked up the knife, snapped the blade shut.

Only now did Chick become aware of the excitement around him—the trail crew crowding in, shouting hoarsely. Yonder, Spud Lantry was staring hard at him with a very peculiar expression on his face. There was the cook's stammered explanation:

"I saw it all, Spud! The guy started after you with a knife, and Bronson tackled him empty-handed."

Someone said, "Hey! You got cut, mister! You're bleedin'!"

"I dunno," mumbled Chick, still dazed. He looked at his knuckles that the knife blade had scraped; he flexed the fingers; The cut hurt a little, but it still did not mean much to him. He fumbled a handkerchief out of his pocket and began trying to wrap it around the hand awkwardly.

"Better help him," Spud Lantry told the cook. "Wash that cut with whisky, just to make sure it ain't infected. I—reckon I'll have to thank you, Bronson," he added, in a chastened voice. "I reckon I didn't miss far having a knife shoved into my back!"

The trail boss turned away before he could answer. Catching sight of the Kansas Kid, looking on with the others, something prompted Spud to add, "Kansas, you're takin' over the woodhawk's chores. Get the ax and get busy!" And without a word the Kid hurried off to his duties.

Somebody said, "What about this thing?"

They had the tramp on his feet now and he stood cowering, speechless, as though waiting for a blow. Spud Lantry gave him a long, cold survey. "Aw, let him go! He can take his crowbait and get out of here, but I don't want ever to lay eyes on him again! Is that plain?" He skewered the man with his hard stare.

The tramp nodded meekly, and as they took their hands from him he turned and shuffled to his horse, fumbled for the stirrup, hauled himself into saddle. In a dead silence he reined around and started away from the circle of firelight.

On an impulse Chick called: "Wait a minute!" and went after him.

The other had halted, looking back with eyes that held fear. "Take your knife," said Chick, drawing it from his pocket. But when he passed it up his hand held something else as well. The tramp felt the crinkle of bills, and his bony face in the firelight took on an odd look.

"Good luck, mister," Chick Bronson told him gruffly. "And watch your step, huh?"

"Thanks!" mumbled the other, as though not quite believing. "Thanks a lot. I'll—remember!"

Then he was gone, into growing darkness. Chick Bronson stood listening for a long time, until the last sound of hoofs had thinned out to silence. Then he turned and walked back, slowly, toward the campfire.

It was a strange world, he was thinking. Damned queer, the way things happened! In a single moment of impulsive action he had saved Spud Lantry's life and put the man in debt to him. It meant there would be no further trouble from Spud—he felt pretty sure of that. It meant that his job with Kimbrough would be assured. The lucky dollar, apparently, still held its charm.

Only there was one thought which occurred to him

and had made him empty his pockets for that poor, addled fellow with the knife. After all, it might have been he! Hunger and despair had driven Chick Bronson pretty far into a corner before inscrutable chance had crossed his trail with that of the doomed Ward McCarey. Given a week or so more, could he say for sure to what desperate madness he might have been driven?

Tonight was a lesson he would not soon forget. It filled him with a deep humility. . . .

EIGHTEEN

The weather had broken sharply. Almost with one stroke the lagging summer ended and real fall was on the range. Frost crackled on a man's blankets as he crawled out of them of a morning. The day they came across the escarpment onto the Lost Wolf yellowed leaves were tearing loose from the cottonwoods and tumbling in a golden shower along the sharp winds under a sky of lumpy gray.

Kimbrough himself wasn't at the ranch, but Bob Creel came slouching out of the big fieldstone house to greet the returning wagon. He looked at Bronson, who had ridden in alongside the trail boss, and turning to Lantry asked, "How did the kid make out?"

"Well enough," said Lantry briefly. His hostility toward Chick had ended after the affair of the attempted knifing, but he was not a man from whom anyone could expect actual friendliness. "So did the

Arrowhead stuff. I'm holding it up on the bench until Kimbrough gives orders to move across the river."

"That's something that may take some doing!"

"More trouble from the Pool?"

"Let's take a pasear over toward the river," said Creel in a sour voice. "I'll show you."

He got his horse and the three of them rode together through the blustering day. Chick Bronson wondered what it was they were to see. He himself was buzzing with questions, anxious to know how matters had been developing in their absence—whether or not anything had turned up yet on the murder of Homer Barnes. But Creel's manner didn't invite probing and he held his silence, troubled.

There was never any escape, he reflected darkly, from a man's problems. During the ordeal of the trail drive, fighting to hold his own against Lantry's jealous dislike, the threat of losing his job had occupied him to the exclusion of everything else. And now that he was back again on the Lost Wolf, it was to find himself caught up once more in the conflicts that tore this range apart.

Where the trail they were following joined the river road, Spud Lantry pulled up suddenly beside a big tree that had a square of cardboard fastened to its trunk, "What the hell's this?" he grunted, and leaned from saddle to hold it steady against the pulling and buffeting of the wind. Past him, Chick Bronson read the placard's printing in cold astonishment:

VOTE!
TO END CORRUPTION
TO END SPECIAL PRIVILEGE
FOR COUNTY JUDGE
MATTHEW FREEDOM

Chick blinked and read it over again. There was more—a block of heavy type describing the candidate as a fearless champion of the rights of the average man—one whose honest integrity and citizenship had never been questioned. There wasn't any picture, but Chick felt sure the only Matthew Freedom he knew of was the frail old-timer at the Lazy F—Josie's grampa.

"Why, of all the damned nerve!" Spud Lantry had seized the placard by one corner, to rip it down, but Creel stopped him.

"Better leave it," the gunman said. "The Pool has got the whole county blanketed with these things—even tacked 'em up on Kimbrough's office in town and the front of the Bull's Head. And the boss won't let anyone touch them."

The range boss demanded, "Why the hell not? They're aimed straight at him! If that old goat can get himself elected in place of Judge Tobias, his next move will be to disallow the Barnes sale and declare it null and void. Kimbrough won't stand by and let them try to put over that sort of trick, will he?"

"He has strange notions sometimes," Creel admitted with a shrug. "He says in a free election it would do more harm to start tearing down the opposition's placards than it would leaving them up for everyone to read. So I guess that's how it'll be."

Spud Lantry scowled, but they rode on without harming the poster. On his part, Chick Bronson allowed himself to feel it was a hopeful sign for the Pool to be willing to settle this issue by a legal test. Election was only two weeks off—altogether a bit late for launching a vigorous campaign. He understood the present occupant of the county bench had held his post for a good many terms without much opposition. So the decision would finally rest on old Matt Freedom's personal reputation and on how much interest his friends could manage to work up.

But where did Ott Stanger fit into this turn of things? Could it be the Pool had broken with him and his violence in favor of peaceful methods? It seemed too much to hope.

Apparently it was. For now they had pulled up on a height commanding a broad view of the tumbling river, and Bob Creel, removing field glasses from his saddle pocket, said, "I want you to take a squint over yonder."

The Lost Wolf was a treacherous, swift-flowing stream between steep banks that leveled in only a few places for an adequate crossing. Just opposite, cresting a rise somewhat lower than this one, was a brushy crown of boulders. Creel pointed, passing the glasses to Lantry. "What do you see?"

"Nothin'." But the range boss quickly amended that. "Wait a minute—there's smoke. Hardly a smudge plain enough to see. Somebody's got him a fire, built small and careful."

"A lookout," Creel explained. "Guarding the crossing—to throw us back if we try it with our beef."

Chick said, "Give 'em here," and Lantry handed the glasses over.

At first, against the dingy sky and blowing wind, he had trouble locating the thin thread of wood smoke marking the lookout's fire. But as he swung the tubes back and forth, hunting, he all at once sighted the man himself—in fact had a good, long look at him as he rose and stood a moment staring down at the swirling river. An exclamation broke from Bronson.

"Why, I know that gent. I mean, I've seen him before. He's not one of the Pool. He was hanging out at Ott Stanger's whisky mill the day I ran into trouble in Hondo Forks."

"So!" Creel returned the glasses to his saddle pocket. "I reckon that ought to answer it! Stanger's called in his own guns. No telling how many are camped yonder on Pool grass."

"It wouldn't have to be a lot," grunted Spud Lantry, "to hold us up. Our hands would be too full with the herd and the river for us to give much of a fight. A few well-placed guns could set a barrage we'd never hope to get through!"

"Then we're stopped—cold. And an easy victory for them! How the devil Stanger was able to bring in his army without our knowing it is more than I can figure, but he's sneaked them in somehow. And licked us in the very first round!" The little gunman picked up the reins, shaking his head. "Nothing to do but report to Kimbrough."

Chick Bronson stirred in the saddle, took a long breath. "I think I got me an idea," he said slowly.

He felt their sharp and skeptical glances; still, they waited for him to continue with the plan that had taken uncertain shape in his mind.

"Stanger caught us off center, and the only way we can hope to counter is to work fast and try to do the same to him. Like you, he'll be figuring there ain't any way Vince Kimbrough can hit back. But now, if we can throw a surprise at him . . ."

"What kind of a surprise?" Bob Creel sounded dubious.

"Well, supposing I was Stanger, now. Supposing I had set up this barricade trap and was waiting for Kimbrough to walk in with his crew and his herd for a general massacre. But supposing, instead, Kimbrough was to hole up on the benches this side of the river and send a single man across by way of the town bridge to take over the Barnes property alone.

"Nobody in particular—in fact, a drifter that I'd had trouble with and had good reason to want to see put in his place. And let's say he brought along with him supplies enough to show he intended staying awhile all by himself. What do you think I'd be apt to do?"

Creel's pale eyes narrowed thoughtfully. "Why, if you was Stanger," he replied slowly, "and this drifter is the man I think you mean, then I imagine you'd count it a made-to-order chance to do just what you wanted with him!"

"And if he turned out to be stubborn about it? Don't you suppose I might lose my head and throw everything I had at this gent—maybe, while I was about it, get a little careless?"

Spud Lantry broke in on him. "In other words, you want to bust Stanger's trap by setting a new one—with yourself as bait?"

"Something like that."

"Kind of a risky job!"

Chick shrugged. "But my job to do—nobody else's. Vince Kimbrough's already announced that he aims for me to run the Barnes property."

Bob Creel was scrubbing his ageless wrinkled face with the fingers of one stubby hand, his eyes clouded as he thought over this program Chick Bronson had suggested. Now he gave his judgment. Picking up the reins, he said bluntly, "I think maybe we better go talk to Vince."

A laden pack horse trailed Chick Bronson's sorrel, and there was a gun in his hand and a queasy, formless discomfort working in his belly as he rode in on the Barnes homestead through afternoon's gray waning light. The lone ride out from town had been an ordeal, knowing peril lay in every turn of the trail. The plan he had conceived and insisted on carrying out with Vince Kimbrough's reluctant concurrence seemed less than wise to him now. But a dogged determination carried him ahead.

He tried to keep his eyes away from that pine limb where he had found Homer Barnes dangling lifeless. Dismounting before the door of the shack, he went in for a quick look around, then came out again and, pocketing his six-gun, proceeded to strip the pack animal of the supplies he had brought. Afterward he turned both horses into the corral and toted his saddle and gear to the house with him.

By the time he had his supplies distributed on shelves behind the wood burner and had tidied up a little the mess the place had been left in, day was pretty well spent. He knew he ought to be hungry but he could find little trace of an appetite; still, he laid a fire in the blackened bowl of the stove and then, as its cheery roar in the chimney began to dispel the chill that lay upon the room, set to work putting together a rudimentary meal.

He had just got a lamp lighted, pushing back the deepening shadows, when he heard riders approaching along the town trail.

Looking around quickly, Chick found a high shelf to place the lamp, where it would not line up his shadow as a target against the room's single window. Then, taking from the bunk the new rifle he had brought with him, he levered a shell into the breech and stepped quickly to the door, placed his shoulder against the wall close beside it.

The horses had jingled to a halt out there in the dust.

A pair of them. Someone called his name uncertainly.

He recognized the voice at once as belonging to Martin Talbot. "Well?" he demanded.

"We want to talk to you, Bronson."

"Who's with you?"

"Josie Freedom," the girl answered for herself.

At that Chick slowly lowered the rifle. There would be no trickery, he felt sure, from these two people. Still, he did not see what good talking would do now, and he hesitated to answer.

Josie Freedom said, "Won't you let us come in? Please!"

He gave in. "All right," he called harshly, and moved away from the door. He was standing with his back to the table, the rifle crooked in the bend of an arm, as saddle leather squealed and then his visitors' steps struck the little porch outside.

The door opened. Josie entered first, and the girl's brown-haired freshness seemed to lighten up that drab place, pulling sharply at Chick despite the strain that was on him. In simple riding skirt and jacket, and plaid shirt opened at her tanned throat, she was prettier even than he had remembered, thinking of her during the lonely days on trail drive. But then Martin Talbot loomed scowling in the doorway behind her, and his presence cut in on these agreeable thoughts.

"Shut the door," Chick Bronson ordered stiffly.

Talbot had colored a little at sight of the weapon in the other's hands. He shoved the door closed and stepped between Chick Bronson and the girl. Pointing at the rifle, he demanded, "Is that the way you greet us when we only wanted to talk?"

"*I* only wanted to talk that night of the meeting," Chick pointed out. "I didn't get much of a welcome then. And after what happened to Homer Barnes, I don't aim to run any risks with the Pool."

"The Pool had nothing to do with what happened to Barnes!" But this only drew Talbot a cold stare of disbelief.

Then Josie Freedom was facing Chick, her head tilted to look up at him, her expression deeply troubled. "We've come to ask—to beg, if necessary—to offer any price within reason, if you'll only pull out of here—tonight—and not force this fight to a showdown! Isn't there any way we can appeal to you?"

"If anyone forces a showdown," he answered sternly, "it will be the Pool—or the hired army you've let Ott Stanger bring in to the Lost Wolf. As long as you people have that to answer for," he added, pressing the point when he thought he saw it strike home, "then you've got no room to talk!"

The girl said, faltering, "I admit Ott Stanger isn't the ally we'd have chosen if there had been a choice. Stanger is a hard man; his methods aren't ours. But they're the same as Vince Kimbrough's, and we're in a spot where we can only hope to fight fire with fire!"

"Is that what you call turning loose a pack of wolves and letting them murder Homer Barnes, simply because he saw fit to follow his own inclinations and not take orders?"

Martin Talbot vented an exclamation of disgust. "Back to that again! Nobody has proved Ott Stanger had any part in what happened to Homer Barnes!"

"Barnes never murdered himself!"

The rancher glared at Chick during a crackling moment of silence. Suddenly he wheeled away, taking Josie Freedom's arm.

"Aw, let's get out of here! You can see there's no talking with this man. I figured it was useless before we tried. But at least we did try! What happens now won't be entirely on our heads!"

"Yeah, I think maybe you'd better be going!" said Chick Bronson. "It's getting later, and me in the midst of supper. Unless I'm plumb mistaken, I should be hearing from Stanger before this night is over. I'd hate to die on an empty belly."

Without any more argument his visitors left him. He stood in chill darkness, listening for long minutes after the sounds of their horses had died along the town trail, leaving only the hiss of pine branches in the rising night wind. It would be a dark night, hardly even a star visible. . . .

Chick Bronson went back into the house, closing the door firmly and dropping the latch into place.

NINETEEN

He first rigged a blanket across each of the windows, as insurance against any unseen lurker stealing up and taking a shot at him unawares. Methodically, then, he finished his preparations and sat down to a lonely meal. He had a small appetite, but nevertheless went through the motions of eating because it gave him something to do. Afterward, having cleaned up after himself, he took his rifle and slipped outside again to test the quality of the night sounds.

There was nothing that might raise alarm. The pair of horses in the corral were quiet. Chick moved about the yard, keeping in dense shadows piled against the wall of the shack and the other buildings, his rifle ready and on the alert for alien movement. So far as he could tell he was alone here. But he was not foolhardy enough to venture into the fringe of the pines.

He returned to the house, put more wood in the stove, and settled to his vigil.

It was lonely enough, and hard enough on nerves stretched taut with apprehension. Chick fished up his old harmonica, thinking to keep himself company with its music, but the doleful strains only made him lonelier. So, instead, finding a battered deck of playing cards that had belonged to Homer Barnes, he sat at the table with six-gun and rifle laid handy and dealt himself hand after hand of solitaire. Mostly he merely turned the cards without seeing them, for all his attention was on the night that lay around that grubby ranch shack and the occasional sounds that drifted in to him.

Yet the night grew older, and nothing happened to disrupt this oppressive quiet. Maybe he had called the play all wrong. Maybe Ott Stanger was not going to rise to the bait. Perhaps he had seen through the trap and hadn't any intention of falling for it.

Perhaps, the thought came with dull horror, Stanger merely figured the upstart drifter had played into his hands now and could be disposed of, any time, at his convenience. Chick Bronson sweated a little over this alarming idea, seeing how surrounded he was here by enemy territory and how far removed from his friends.

After a while his hands felt stiff and numb as he turned the cards, and he realized he had nearly let the fire in the stove go out. He rose and stuck in a few lengths of pitch pine, saw the tongues of dying flame revive before he closed it up. The hour, he judged, was late; the endless, keyed-up waiting was telling on him severely. This had been a long day too. Perhaps it would be a good idea to hit the bunk, stretch out, and try to force taut nerves to lessen. He hardly thought there was much danger he would fall asleep.

He was reaching for the lamp upon the shelf to turn it down when he heard the shrill neighing of a horse somewhere in the pine trees.

Quickly he blew the lamp and stood like that a moment, scarcely breathing, but catching no further sound. Still, what he had heard was enough. It hadn't been either of his own horses, running in the night corral; the noise hadn't come from that direction. And it had ended as abruptly as if a man's hand, descending upon the muzzle of the horse, had chopped the whinny short. A man somewhere out there in the night and the trees.

With the lamp extinguished, the dance of fire in the stove box filtered through its cracks to lay many busy shadows upon the walls and a kind of half-light. It glinted on the weapons waiting handy on the table top. Chick snatched up the six-gun, shoved it into his waistband. Then, hefting the rifle, he moved quickly to a window and lifted a corner of the blanket.

Dimly he could make out the open space of the ranch yard and the dark wall of pines beyond— nothing else, though he stared until his eyes began to smart and he had to blink them hard. Leaving that window, he drifted over to the second, and immediately picked up a red speck of fire, glowing against the blackness.

At once the six-gun was in his hand, and he struck the windowpane a slashing blow with its barrel. And as the glass went out, sharply shattering, he laid a shot in the direction of that fool with the lighted cigarette.

The blast of the gun raised a squawk from somewhere in the trees; next instant a quick barrage of fire began rattling along the edge of the timber, spoiling the night quiet. Lead hammered the shack like hail. Chick Bronson had dropped to the floor with the first volley and he crouched there, stunned a little by the storm he had touched off.

They were outside all right! Scattered through the trees, they had the ranch surrounded. Chick's unexpected shot must have startled them and begun things prematurely, for as this run of answering fusillade played out and died, the voice of Ott Stanger could be heard shouting angrily, "Hold your fire, damn it! Hold it!"

Now, why? Chick wondered, and next instant thought he knew the answer. That loot of Ward McCarey's! Of course! He had entirely forgotten, but it was plain the other man hadn't. Stanger still held firm to his belief that Chick Bronson knew its hiding place, and it must be this supposed knowledge, complicating things, that necessitated he be taken alive.

The thought raised his confidence, turned him suddenly a trifle cocky. For if his enemies weren't privileged to draw blood, there was certainly no such restraint on him! Raising himself again, he reached up and gave the blanket window covering a yank that jerked it free. Outside, the pines seemed alive with moving shadows, and he threw off a quick pair of shots, almost at random.

The abruptness with which they drew a fire sent him ducking again, his newborn cockiness already shaken. Maybe they weren't so particular, after all, about not killing him!

Now this flurry, too, threaded out and ended. Crouched beneath the window, in flickering firelight,

Chick Bronson fumbled shells from his coat pocket to replace the ones he had emptied. Out in the night pen he heard the frenzied neighing of his horses, frightened by the tumult of guns.

Suddenly Ott Stanger's voice sounded again—this time calling the besieged man's name. Chick hesitated a long minute before answering, and when he did he had to swallow and clear his tight throat of burnt powder sting before he could manage even a hoarse sound. "Yeah?"

"Kid, I'm giving you a chance to surrender. If you're not a complete fool you'll take it."

"You can go to blazes!" Chick Bronson retorted with a confidence he was actually a long way from knowing. "Vince Kimbrough set me here to run this property for him, and I figure I'll hang and rattle awhile!"

"Big talk!" snarled a voice that he recognized as Ed Dugan's. Still, there was silence for a moment, as if the men outside did not know quite how to answer such defiance.

When Stanger spoke again it was to try a different tack, of persuasion. "It just don't make sense—throwin' away your hide for no better cause than this! Tell me, kid! What's Kimbrough paying you? Name his figure, and I'll up it!"

This offer was the last thing Chick had expected. It frankly staggered him. "*You?*"

"Sure! I admire spunk. You've given me a lot of trouble, but I'm willing to forget if you'll just switch over and put an end to all this nonsense."

"You want to forget about Ward McCarey's loot while you're at it?" demanded Chick Bronson boldly.

This seemed to catch Stanger up short, for there was a moment wherein no answer came from the dark trees. Then he said harshly, "We can make a deal, I reckon. Let me come in so we can talk terms."

"Sorry! No deals, Stanger! I'd talk to the Pool, but I don't reckon you've got any of them out there. They're decent enough people, even if they are fools enough to throw in with such a bunch of snakes!"

Ott Stanger cursed wildly. "You figure to make a stand, do you? Why, you poor simp, you don't really think we'd let the likes of you hold us up? We're coming in!"

"Come ahead!" shouted Chick. And the attack had started.

From one window to another Chick Bronson ran, stripping down blankets, smashing out glass with his gun barrel. Cold air swirled in, and with it gun sound and the yells of men rushing toward the cabin. Kicking the door wide open, he knelt and slapped rifle stock to cheek, threw off a half-dozen shots as fast as he could flip the lever.

Out of the trees dark figures were breaking in a long skirmish line; guns answered his fire. His bullets slowed the charge from that direction, however, and immediately he was up and running to a window, crouched low to clear the bullets that screamed overhead. Again he fired a burst, targeting powder spark; again hurried to a new post.

156

Fear and despair were a hard knot inside his belly. One man could not hold off a four-direction charge against ruthless men bent on eliminating him. They were closing in now, ducking and dodging across the ranch yard, converging on this shack from all directions as they drew their noose of bullets closer.

He shot the rifle dry and hurled it from him, bringing out the six-gun. There was no time to reload. Boots struck the stoop beyond the doorway and he whirled, threw off a bullet that swept the opening clear. But they were that close. Another moment, and they'd have him. . . .

Where were Creel, and Lantry, and the others? What had become of the trap so carefully planned?

He had his answer then in a sudden withering fusillade of gunfire that broke from the timber fringe, catching the attackers from behind. It was beautifully timed, brilliantly executed. Stanger's men could have had no inkling that their enemies were moving in, drawing a second line of guns around the one they had placed about the ranch. Now, caught in the open with no cover from this surprise attack, they were thrown in an instant into yelling, terrified confusion.

Just once Chick heard Ott Stanger's voice, trying to rally his men and whip some order into them, but it was already too late. They were being beaten down by the uneven odds, their guns quickly silencing. A few made a desperate rush for the protection of the shack, but Chick Bronson held these off, working his six-gun until its hammer hit an empty cylinder. With hurrying, trembling fingers he shook out the used shells, fumbled new ones from his pocket and stuffed them in, clicked the loading gate shut.

By that time the whole thing was over.

Firing broke off, straggled out to a few last, meaningless shots, and after that, silence that left a man's ears throbbing. Voices called back and forth across the ranch yard, cautiously approaching—there was always a danger someone might be playing 'possum, pretending to be dead, waiting his chance to leap and break for the trees.

Chick Bronson moved away from the wall where he stood, and in the numbing quiet of aftermath his knees were almost too shaky to support him. He gained the door, sagging there limply to stare out upon the slaughter. There was little enough to see in that poor light after the blinding of powder flash—a few dark shapes huddled grotesquely; others converging, afoot, across the yard some leading boogered horses.

Then a voice spoke near by, and Bob Creel was beside him with a smoking gun dragging from his fist.

"You all right, kid?"

He was somewhat surprised to discover that he was. Some lead had drilled pretty close to him, but none had tallied—not even for a minor scratch. "A couple minutes more," he said, "and I dunno!"

"It was cutting it fine," Creel admitted. "We had to be mighty careful moving in. We figured Stanger knew it would be impossible to bring cattle across the river by night, but just the same we couldn't be sure of not running into a rear guard."

Now Vince Kimbrough joined them. To Creel he said, "Better take charge, Bob. The boys are rounding up prisoners and checking over the dead, to see exactly what we've bagged. We smashed them completely, though in the dark it's likely that some slipped past. We just have to be sure Stanger wasn't among them!"

"I got you!"

Creek hurried off, and Kimbrough turned to Chick. "Well, boy," he said gently, "you did your piece, and did it well! I'm pretty proud of you. Now let's go inside and get a lamp lighted, and add up the totals of just what we've accomplished tonight!"

TWENTY

In only one respect the tally proved disappointing. Neither Ott Stanger nor Ed Dugan appeared to be among the gun toughs slain or taken in the battle. A double check under Bob Creel's close supervision made this clear beyond question. "They got through our hands somehow," he said, his wrinkled features scowling, "and in the night there's small hope of running them down."

Kimbrough took the news soberly but philosophically. "Not long till daybreak," he pointed out. "As soon as it's light enough we'll take the trail. If they're still in the valley we'll find them!" He looked at Chick

Bronson. "You're quite sure Stanger was out there tonight?"

"Plenty sure," said Chick. "And Dugan too." He was so near exhaustion it was an effort for his lips and tongue to form words.

"All right." To Creel, Kimbrough added, "Meanwhile, get somebody to brew up some coffee. We all can use it. And if any of the boys collected bullet wounds during that ruckus, see what can be done about them. We'll send them into town, along with the prisoners."

With the first filtering of dawn they started out—a grim calvalcade of horsemen, armed and ready, and determined to finish the job that had been nearly completed that night. It was a bleak gray morning under a low ceiling of scudding cloud in a wind-filled sky. Moving out across the slick carpeting of cured brown grass, they rode with weapons ready, not knowing what they might find waiting for them.

What they found was a deserted and silent range. Herds in the various Pool brands moved across the bottoms but there was no sign of a rider; and the ranch headquarters themselves, when they sighted them, were desolate and without movement. There might have been no other living soul except this line of horsemen sweeping slowly eastward and riding high in stirrups as they scanned the valley flats.

Bob Creel, riding between Vince Kimbrough and Chick, ventured his own opinion. "They're lying low! Maybe none of the Pool was in that bust-up last night,

but they know damn well what happened. They kn̸
they're licked, with no imported gun hands left ̸
stand between them and us.

"Stanger may be hiding on one of these ranches,"
Kimbrough said. "We'll search them all if we have
to!"

They approached the first, spread out and ready to
flush the quarry they sought. They rode to within a
dozen yards of the buildings before Kimbrough sig-
naled a halt, and still roused no sign of life though
they kept a careful lookout for the gleam of a hidden
gun barrel. Smoke rose from the kitchen chimney,
however; the place was not deserted.

At last the door cracked open narrowly. A man's
face, gray with fear, showed there. "What do you want
with us?"

"Nothing," Kimbrough answered. "Unless you're
hiding Ott Stanger. Him we want."

"Ain't seen him."

Kimbrough considered, then shook his head. "I
think we'll have to look for ourselves. Don't make
trouble. If you're telling the truth, neither you nor any
of your family will be harmed. If you're not—then
God help you!"

The Pool rancher started a protest, choked it off as
he saw the fruitlessness of it. At Kimbrough's order he
came out of the house and his family followed him. In
sullen silence they stood and watched while a detail
headed by Bob Creel swung down and made the
search.

They turned up nothing, in house or barn or any of the outbuildings. Bob Creel ordered them impatiently back into saddle.

But before reining away Vince Kimbrough spoke a last reminder to the frightened Pool rancher. "From the beginning I've tried to make you people see I wanted no trouble. You insisted on war and let Stanger bring in an army to fight it for you. Now that army is smashed, and I hope we can have an end to this foolish wrangling!"

The other's mouth worked with emotion. "There's still an election coming!" he blurted.

Kimbrough considered this for a moment, then he was turning away abruptly, nodding to his men. The cavalcade filed out of the yard.

On they went, eastward across the reaches of the valley floor, while the sun climbed higher—a greasy smear behind clouds that scudded above the rim. Nowhere did they meet any opposition. And then, at last, a scout returned with the first real evidence as to what had become of the men they were seeking.

In the dust of the rim road they examined prints, hours old, that had been made by galloping, hard-pushed mounts, and immediately Spud Lantry said, "That's it! That's Stanger, heading out as fast as he could cover ground! He and Dugan will be clean gone by now—and not stopping this side of Hondo Forks!"

They all looked at Kimbrough, awaiting his decision. He studied the sign with eyes hooded behind heavy lids; straightened, lifting his shoulders.

"So much for Ott Stanger. He's through. After such a beating as he took last night, I wager he'll never again raise the men or the nerve to tackle the Lost Wolf! We've had victory enough; we can forget him!" Kimbrough looked around at his men, all of them drawn and blear-eyed from sleeplessness and strain.

"We ride back now. This will do for one day."

Spud Lantry asked quickly, "What about the Arrowhead stuff, boss? Nobody can stop us now from putting it across the river onto Pool graze. Say the word and we start moving."

"No." Kimbrough slowly shook his head, drawing Spud's look of surprise.

"Why the hell not? They're licked. We can move right in and no one will lift a hand to stop us."

"Maybe. But remember what that man told us. There's still the election—only two weeks off. We can roughshod over these people and risk a general war, and it could boomerang against us; maybe even help lose us the judgeship race. And you know what that could mean.

"No, we'll hold off now that we're rid of Stanger. We'll make no further move until we see how well Matt Freedom does at the polls. If he loses, there'll be nothing more to worry about."

Bob Creel said ominously. "And if he wins? You know the Pool is putting a lot of effort into this campaign!"

His chief shrugged tiredly inside the loose-hanging sack coat. "It's a free country. Anyway, we'll have to think about that when the time comes." Turning to Chick Bronson then, Kimbrough said, "You look worn out, boy. Ride on to town with us and get some sleep. I'll send someone to bring the pack horse in and close the Barnes shack until after election."

Tired as he was, Chick Bronson made a quick objection. "I don't aim to sit around doing nothing for two weeks. I want to earn my keep."

"We can talk about that later," Vince Kimbrough said briefly. "Right now let's be getting back."

Chick Bronson had never been so tired. Hitting town, he took care of his sorrel and then, not able to give a thought to food or anything else, went to the hotel and tumbled into a bed without shedding more than his boots. He was asleep immediately, and when he awoke sometime in late afternoon he had not once changed position.

He poured water into the basin on the washstand and doused his face in it, letting its coldness cut through the fog of exhaustion that clouded his brain. Afterward, feeling more like himself, he shaved, toweling vigorously, and then stomped into his boots, got hat and jacket, and went down to put some food into his hollow belly.

When he entered the Bull's Head a little later he found the barroom nearly deserted, the tables pushed back and chairs ranked on top of them while the place was swept out and damp sawdust scattered over the plank floor. Chick bought a drink and was finishing it leisurely, leaning against the bar, when Vince Kimbrough entered through the batwings.

"Oh, hello there," said Kimbrough. "I was about to go over to the hotel and see if you had waked up yet. How do you feel?"

"Well, at least I'm awake," Chick Bronson admitted, grinning. "You wanted me for something?"

"Have another drink."

But the younger man declined, not being much of a drinking man. Kimbrough said, "In that case, I suppose we might as well be getting along to the sheriff's office. You said something about wanting to keep busy the next couple of weeks before election, and as it happens Mart Murray needs a man for some routine county business. When he spoke to me just now, I naturally thought of you."

"What's the job?"

"Murray will explain. Shall we go?"

Passing along the empty wind-scoured street, they encountered a good many of the Pool's election placards, plastered upon building fronts and roof-support posts, all bearing Matthew Freedom's blatant challenge to corruption and dishonesty in the county government. Chick gave his boss a sidelong look, trying to decipher what reaction these things brought in Kimbrough, but the lean, brooding face held nothing readable. Finally he blurted:

"Don't they make you sore at all—smeared all over town, even nailed on the door of your office, and the Bull's Head?"

Kimbrough looked at him with surprise. "Why should they? That's politics, my boy; and any man has the right to promote his candidates."

"What do you think of Freedom's chances?"

"We'll find out, come election day. His supporters are working hard, but he's not much known outside the valley and there's a lot of ground to be covered."

They turned up the wide steps of the courthouse. Entering, they passed an individual in a rusty frock coat and drooping string tie who nodded solemnly behind the pince-nez that rode his high-bridged nose. His skin was a sickly yellow color, and he walked with an elaborate, unsteady dignity. A pungent cloud of whisky fumes floated about him that wrinkled Chick Bronson's nose.

"Judge Tobias," remarked Kimbrough dryly. "You know, maybe at that he has been in office too long! Maybe a little competition is going to be good for him."

Mart Murray sat at the desk in his office. A cane was hooked over the arm of the sheriff's swivel chair, ready to his hand, and he indicated it. "Pardon me for not gettin' up. Bronc fell on me a couple days ago, hurt my hip. So I'm getting caught up on my desk work."

Preliminaries over, he opened a drawer, brought out a bundle of vouchers wrapped with a rubber band and tossed them into Chick's lap.

"Delinquent taxes," he explained. "It's part of my job to collect them, but I can't do much the way I'm bunged up just now, and it'll soon be time for the new assessments to be made. Vince thought you might like to try your hand." He added, "You get a percentage of everything you bring in; it makes pretty good pay."

Chick Bronson considered, thumbing through the vouchers doubtfully. "Well, I suppose I could take a stab at it."

"Just collect what you can," said Murray, "and when you've gone through those I'll have some more ready to work on. Remember, though, don't get too rough! Makes a bad impression, you know, in an election year."

"I can understand that." Chick fingered the vouchers a moment longer, and then stuffed them into a pocket. "O.K.," he said, rising. "I'll do my best. They'll probably sick the dogs on me, but I should have got used to that, riding grub-line. This, at least, is an improvement!"

They shook hands, and a moment later Chick Bronson walked out of the gloomy courthouse to assume his new duties as a tax collector.

"Anyway," he told himself, "I'll never say I've been in a rut since I hit this country!"

The new job quickly proved to be an education in itself—a grim sort of initiation into other people's problems. For he soon learned how badly hard times had hit this country, putting a lot of folk behind on their taxes and not many owning the cash to pay. Several swore at Chick Bronson when he rode up and announced his purpose; a few invited him to sit with them over a bottle of rye while they went into a dolorous account of the reasons why they couldn't pay.

Once, in the roughs below the headwaters of the Lost Wolf, a gaunt, tired-faced woman, whose husband had died and left her with three kids and a hardscrabble homestead to manage, stood before him in the door of her shack and cried while a whimpering baby clung to her shabby skirts. That time Chick did some fast figuring of the money in his own pocket and what percentage he had due him, and before he rode away from there he had surreptitiously marked the widow's voucher "PAID."

"I can't do *that* often," he told himself sourly, "or I'll end up losing my shirt!" But at least the job was opening his eyes to the fact that other folks had their problems, too, and that in abnormal times like these a drifting grub-liner had no business considering himself the sole, mistreated victim of chance and of other men's greedy indifference. Everybody was in this particular boat. . . .

He covered a lot of miles, hunch-shouldered into his windbreaker while the weather turned steadily colder. This county was a good-sized one, even as western counties went, though not all of it so fertile or so well-populated as the Lost Wolf Valley which formed its heart.

Then one day the sheriff handed him a voucher with the comment, "This one may be dynamite. Handle it careful." He looked at the name and the amount of delinquency, and vented a low whistle.

It was Matt Freedom's voucher, and the tax due was a sizable one—the largest he had yet been called on to collect.

"That's right off the books," Murray answered his question with a shrug. "It's what he owes all right. And I think you'll be doing damn well to get any of it out of him!"

With deep misgivings Chick Bronson stowed the voucher away inside his coat and went out and climbed into the saddle. Though he had every reason in the world for dreading this chore, it was a thing that had to be done.

A strong wind pushed at him, blowing down from the rim, as he struck out along the looping wagon trail through the bunch grass toward the Lazy F.

TWENTY-ONE

Smoke, buffeted by a whipping wind, rose from the kitchen chimney to dispel a momentary hope that he would find no one home here, and resignedly Chick jogged his sorrel in toward the little clot of buildings. As he drew nearer he became aware of the rhythmic strokes of an ax at a woodpile behind the house. He rode around there, to discover Josie Freedom, in jeans and a hickory shirt, knocking up a little pile of split kindling.

The girl saw him coming and straightened slowly, grounding the heavy ax while she stared at him without welcome. A sudden gust of the wind that tumbled down the slope behind the ranch eddied about them both, snapping at the brim of Chick's hat, swirling Josie's brown curls until she put up a hand to trap them and keep them from her face. He couldn't help but notice how the wind molded the bulky material of the shirt against her firm young body, accenting its shape charmingly.

"What do you want?" she prompted him, her voice holding no warmth.

Reluctantly Chick Bronson brought himself to the object of his mission. "Your grandfather," he said. "I'd like to talk to him, if he's available."

There was a hesitation, just perceptible, before she answered, with a jerk of her head toward the barn, "Over there."

"Thanks."

He gave the sorrel a nudge in that direction, noting that the girl had left her ax leaning against the woodpile and was following. As he dismounted stiffly, he saw old Matt Freedom toss a pitchfork aside and walk forward to meet him in the doorway, a suspicious look on his bearded face.

"Don't tell me!" the old man grunted. "We heard you was running tax vouchers around for Vince Kimbrough's sheriff, but I know you haven't got one for us. We're all paid up."

Chick had been fumbling in his pocket. The old man's flat assurance made him blink, halting him for a moment; then, slowly, he drew out the paper and held it toward Matt Freedom.

He said, "Not according to the records you ain't, Mr. Freedom. I got orders to hand you this."

A medley of expressions ran across the old man's face—surprise, incredulity, and then a slow building of anger. All at once Matt Freedom's eyes were ablaze, his bloodless lips trembling. "Why, the filthy, stinkin' gall—"

"Grampa!" cried Josie sharply.

With a convulsive gesture Freedom snatched the paper from Chick's hand, peered at it. Chick Bronson said uneasily, "Of course, now, if you think there's been a mistake, Mr. Freedom—"

"Mistake!" the old man's voice shook; his bony hands, his entire frail body, were tense with wrath. "A deliberate lie—that's what it is! Unfair as the taxes are in this county, I've known it was no use protesting. But—this— Why, the sheer brazen effrontery of those crooked—" He crumpled the paper sharply in his fingers.

The girl cried, "Let's see, Grandpa!" She came and took the voucher from him, and as she looked at the figures her frown deepened.

Chick Bronson wished he could have been elsewhere just then. He said anxiously, "Now wait a minute! You understand I don't know anything about these assessments—I just try to collect them. But if your taxes are paid, there certainly should be a way to prove it. You've got the receipts, haven't you?"

"Some of them." The old man shrugged bitterly,

subsiding a little. "What good will they do, if the county records have been tampered with?"

"That I just can't believe," said Chick stubbornly. Yet as soon as the words were spoken they sounded lame to him. All at once he wasn't quite so sure.

Josie Freedom said, "But what are we going to do? Have we enough money to pay?"

"Yeah—just!" the old man said. "Only, we aren't going to. Not a dime! It's a dirty steal, that's all!"

"Just the same," Chick told him impulsively, "fair or not, you want to remember that you're running for office. Would it help your chances if word got around that you refused to pay a tax?"

The old man's brow lowered as he stabbed a keen look at the other. He began to nod thoughtfully, and one thin claw of a hand came up to work at the long whiskers.

"By gonnies!" Matt Freedom exclaimed. "I think you've named it, boy! That's it! They've done this a-purpose, just to rile me into some move that could be used to smear me with the voters!"

His jaw hardened then in deliberation. "All right, I'll cross 'em up. I'll pay the damn thing. It'll take every cent of hard cash we own, but if I can manage to nail the election, I swear that that cesspool of a county courthouse is gonna see a cleanin' out like it's never had! Wait here a minute," he added. "I got the money inside the house. I'll bring it out to you."

He went pegging away, returning after a long moment while the two young people waited out in a stilted silence—Chick fiddling with his rein ends and scuffing an elaborate pattern in the dust with his boot toe, Josie hugging herself against the chill which she was undoubtedly feeling, now that she had stopped exercising with the ax. They were both relieved when Matt came back, a wad of bills in his fist.

"Here!" he grunted. "Count it, to make sure my end of this transaction is perfectly complete and above-board, and then give me a receipt. It'll be the club to whack my enemies with when the time comes!"

Solemnly Chick went through the formalities. Afterward, with the money in his pocket, he touched hat-brim briefly to Josie Freedom and reached again for the reins of his sorrel, wanting nothing now but to get away. But a word from the old man checked him.

"One moment, fellow." Matt sounded puzzled and apologetic. "I'm thinking I may have misjudged you some, after all. You've talked pretty straight about this business. I mustn't forget you're a newcomer to the Lost Wolf and maybe so not actually a party to the wickedness that goes on here."

"Look, Mr. Freedom," said Chick impulsively, and his words were as much for the girl as for her grand-father. "A man has to eat, and he owes loyalty to the gent that pays him wages. But I'm caught right in the middle of something that I don't much like. You're an honest man; that much I'm sure of. And yet you call my boss a crook, which I find it impossible to believe!"

The old man's bearded head bobbed slowly.

"I think perhaps I understand. Vince Kimbrough is one slick talker, doggone smooth and honest-sounding when he has an impression he wants to make. You just haven't been around him long enough to see behind that mask he wears. But one of these days you're bound to see, and I only hope when that day comes you'll remember that we tried to warn you!"

Chick Bronson took this in silence, then, because no answer suggested itself, he merely nodded and, turning to his waiting mount, lifted into saddle. It was with a sense of relief that he rode away from that awkward meeting; but long after the Lazy F was left behind a swirl of confused and troubled thoughts rode with him.

A horseman came out of the trees that rimmed a low ridge ahead and quartered down toward the trail, a hand lifted shortly in greeting. It was Bob Creel, he saw, not without surprise; you didn't often find Creel out on the trails this far from town and Kimbrough's headquarters. Creel hauled up, firing a cigarette, and as the other man drew even he flipped out the match and said casually, "Still riding the rounds, huh? How's collections?"

"Not good," Chick answered shortly. "Times are too tough."

"They'll get better."

Creel nudged his bronc forward and fell in beside Chick, and they went on along the trail at an easy walk. There was no discussion of how the gunman had happened to be there, or where they both were heading now; they talked a little of indifferent matters.

Presently, and unconnected with anything else that had been said, Creel asked: "You've been to the Freedoms'?" And at Chick's nod: "The old man pay up all right?"

Something jarred Chick like a blow. He turned slowly, laid his look squarely upon the wrinkled, ageless face. It was, he saw, as inscrutable as ever, the slate-blue eyes veiled and empty of meaning. But the question itself had betrayed him; it had told Chick everything he needed to know.

Trying to keep his voice from trembling, his hands steady on the reins, Chick answered, "Sure he paid. But he wasn't supposed to, was he? It was meant for a frame-up—a political trap!"

This brought him Creel's full attention at last; tore away for an instant the curtain from the cautious, probing stare. The man covered up again quickly, pulling his glance away from Chick to study the half-smoked quirly butt that he plucked from his thin, flat lips. But they both had halted their mounts unconsciously, and they sat motionless now with the wind whooping and booming around them.

"This Freedom," Bob Creel murmured, still considering the glowing end of his hand-rolled cigarette. "You know, kid, it could mean trouble for all of us if he should happen to win the election. Most likely the boss would lose the Barnes place and his toehold this side of the river. But you've thought of that, I reckon."

"Sure," said Chick bitterly. "I guess I got brains enough to figure that out for myself, at least!"

"Maybe we could appeal the decision," the other man went on. "But we can't count on it. And of course you understand that if Vince loses the Barnes place he won't be able to give you the job he planned to, managing it for him. In fact, kid," Bob Creel pointed out very softly, "you very possibly might wind up without any job at all."

This time Chick Bronson kept silent, waiting to see what the man was coming to. He knew this was all a preparation for something.

"Still, maybe there's a way out," Creel said, "a little more drastic than our first idea, of letting Freedom put himself in a bad light by refusing to pay his taxes. But if it worked it should be enough to tie his hands until the election is over. I guess it's up to you, kid."

"Why? What do I have to do?"

"Not a lot, really. Just give me the money Freedom paid you, and then ride back to town and tell the sheriff you've had a stickup. Somebody waylaid you—you couldn't see his face, because he kept out of sight behind a pile of rock with only the top of his hat and his gun barrel showing. But you recognized his voice, all right—it was Freedom's!

"That ought to sew up the election for us! Afterward, of course, when the danger's over, you can decide that you might have been mistaken and you can't swear it was Freedom's voice you heard. The sheriff will turn the old fellow loose for lack of evidence; no one will have been hurt at all, really. How does it sound?"

Chick Bronson felt a numbness all through him. "It sounds like you and Kimbrough have got everything figured!" He added: "So I think you must have gone and worked out a third scheme too, just in case I didn't care for the second one?"

"Why, yes, we did," Bob Creel told him evenly. "Count on Vince Kimbrough to figure all the angles— like having us string up Homer Barnes to keep him from carrying out his threat of reneging on that sale, and at the same time make it look like Ott Stanger's doings!"

The world seemed to be reeling under Bronson's saddle. "*You* killed Barnes?"

"Sure." The wrinkled face broke into a grin of sneering amusement. "And now it looks like I'll have to testify that I saw Matt Freedom kill you, trying to take back his money."

Twisting sharply in saddle, Chick made a grab for the arm that had brought Creel's six-gun sliding smoothly out of holster. Muscle, like taut steel wire; strained beneath his fingers as they struggled for the weapon, both silent except for the grunt of panting breath. Creel's efforts to pull free nearly lifted Chick from his saddle, but he knew it meant his life, and he clung with everything he had, meanwhile working desperately to reach Ott Stanger's silver-handled Colt in the deep pocket of his windbreaker.

He got his hand on it but the hammer spur dug into the cloth and stuck there, unyielding when he tried to yank it loose. And now, all at once, the horses veered apart; they both went out of leather, spilling bodily into the trail, and in the impact Chick lost all hold on his opponent.

TWENTY-TWO

He hurled himself at Creel, but the latter had rolled out of the way and now was scrambling to his feet, the gun leveling. And Chick, lunging up from the ground, went after him recklessly. He had to forget his own trapped gun in the effort to keep Creel from using his. And in fact he only managed to knock the other's hand aside in time to send a bullet drilling past him.

Chick felt the heat of the muzzle flash, the kick of concussion. His right fist struck wildly, then, and landed in the center of Creel's dark and wrinkled face, causing the man to stumble a step backward. But Creel was a wiry, quick-moving man; he caught his footing and he swung a clubbing blow with the hand that held the gun.

Throwing up an arm, Chick blocked it, but the smashing of the barrel nearly numbed his whole left side. He gritted his teeth against this pain, countered with a wild, looping right. Luckily it connected. It took his opponent full in the jaw and sent him clear around and into the dirt.

The smoking gun spilled from Bob Creel's fingers; Chick booted it away and then stood waiting, panting and ready for the other to reach his feet. Creel was a little slow doing it. And as soon as he had his boots under him Chick Bronson hammered him down again.

Bob Creel was a gun fighter, strictly, with small skill in using his fists, while Chick had taken part in enough bunkhouse brawls to know how to look out for himself, at least against an opponent anywhere near his own size. Moreover, he had the weight of righteous anger on his side now.

There might have been time, during one of these moments while he waited for Creel to come back at him, to have cleared the gun trapped in his pocket, but somehow he didn't even think of it. Some primitive instinct had wakened in Chick, and he wanted to use his hands, to strike and hurt. Someone had to pay for the way in which, as he now knew, he had been duped by Creel, and by Vince Kimbrough, and used to further their greedy ends.

When Bob Creel's nose smashed beneath his fist and he felt the warm blood spurt, Chick drew from this a profound, savage satisfaction. And moments later Creel went plowing on head and shoulders into the dust of the trail and that time he stayed there, a thoroughly beaten man.

Slowly Chick's mind began to clear itself of the black fumes of anger. At last, wiping his bloody hands on the cloth of his jeans, he turned away and leaned to pick up the hat that he had lost in the battle; shoving the hair out of his sweaty face, he dragged it on. The emotional aftermath was sudden and complete, leaving him shaky in the knees and drained of feeling.

Bob Creel had pushed up to a sitting position, blood

dripped from his battered nose as he stared glassily at the man who had bested him. His mouth twisted and he grunted, "You damn punk."

Not answering, Chick Bronson walked over and picked up the gun he'd kicked away from the other's hand, stood dangling it by the trigger guard as he made up his mind. He went then to where the two horses, after spooking briefly, had fallen to grazing beside the trail, and caught up the reins. He tied the captured gun to Creel's saddle strings.

The gunman, watching, showed the first sign of alarm. "What do you think you're doing?" he demanded.

Chick looked at him. "I'd be within my rights to kill you," he said. "Instead, I'm only gonna set you afoot. You'll have a nice cold walk back to town. After that, the fun of explaining everything to Vince Kimbrough. That ought to just about square our account."

"You'd better kill me!" gritted the other. "Because when I do get my hands on a horse and a gun—"

Chick shrugged. "I'll be long gone from here by that time, I reckon. I want to forget I ever set eyes on this Lost Wolf country. I've let myself be played for a sucker from the day I hit it, and there's no fun in bein' reminded of how many kinds of a damn fool a guy has been!"

"You were pretty green, all right," said Creel, his pale eyes narrowing with scorn. "That first night you showed up at the Bull's Head, wet as a drowned rat and flashing Ward McCarey's hoodooed coin, the boss

180

spotted you as something he could use. He's made good use of you too."

"But for the last time!" Chick turned to his sorrel and went up into leather, and he took the bridle reins of the other horse. Bob Creel came stumbling to his feet, moving forward as though to stop him, but he held up in his tracks when Chick showed him the muzzle of the gun which he finally had yanked free of his windbreaker's pocket.

"Just stay back!" Chick warned. "I'll take no more chances with you!"

Creel's angry swearing followed him as he rode away from there, the second mount trailing.

When he had covered a couple of miles he turned the other horse adrift, with a smart slap of rein ends across the rump to set it heading for its stall in town. Bob Creel would be doing well on foot, if he staggered in by midnight at the earliest, and this should give Chick plenty of time to get a start out of the valley.

He didn't know yet which way he would be riding—somewhere down the hopeless grub-line trail that he had dared to believe was left behind him. At least there was a little money in his pocket, accumulated from the few weeks' pay he'd managed to tally with Vince Kimbrough.

Suddenly he recalled that other wad of bills, and fished it out—Matt Freedom's tax money. He frowned, reminded of so many things that had passed between him and those folks at the Lazy F: the times they had tried in vain to warn him, to make him see the facts about the men he had got himself hooked up with. He should have known enough to believe them from the start.

Chick pocketed the bills again and kicked his sorrel forward. Lazy F was the last spread you passed on the main trail leaving the valley. At least Matt Freedom should have back this money of which he had nearly been cheated.

At the sound of a rider entering the yard, the house door was thrown open and Josie Freedom came hurrying out, but she halted in her tracks when she saw who the visitor was. He saw puzzlement and anger and fear all mingled in her pretty face. Sharply she demanded, "What do you want now? Haven't you done enough to us?"

Leaning from saddle, he held out to her the wad of money. "Here," he said. And when she hesitated, merely staring at him without making a move to accept it, "Please! Just take this—and don't ask any questions."

"But I don't understand," she exclaimed. "Is this another of Vince Kimbrough's tricks?"

Chick Bronson took a deep breath. So there were going to have to be explanations, after all. "It's not a trick," he answered dully. "I finally woke up to the truth of what you and your grandfather have been trying to tell me." He related as much of his encounter with Bob Creel as he needed to, and of the lie he had been asked to swear to.

"I was a damn fool," he ended. "But before I check out of this country I had to return the money I took from you. Since you have the receipt, they can't try to collect their phony tax a second time. They'll have to think up something else!"

She took the money now, but automatically, without looking at it. Her eyes on Chick's face, she said, "You're leaving the Lost Wolf?"

"Driftin' out—the way I came," he agreed bitterly. "Why not? If I could do anything to counteract the harm I've caused, I might stay. But I'd only make worse mistakes; and you don't need any saddle bums around the place."

She misunderstood his meaning, however. "We'd have no right to ask you," she said, thinking she knew what was in his mind. "It's not your fight, and Kimbrough or Bob Creel would surely kill you if you stayed. But thank you for bringing the money back, anyway. I've got to ride now, and find Grampa—he headed for Martin's place as soon as you left. He was going to call the rest of the Pool together. He was terribly worked up."

Chick watched her turn away and hurry toward the tack room in the barn. At least, he thought, she seemed to hold no hard feelings against him for the mistakes he had made. That was something.

He ran a hand across his face. He was still tired from the fight with Creel, his throat and mouth parched, his head a little giddy. Reining over toward the well, he swung down to get himself a drink before taking his last leave of this valley and its tangled affairs.

Josie came out of the barn, her arms laden with riding gear, and saw him turning the winch. "That well went dry a year ago," she called. "If you want water, I'll fetch you some from the pump in the kitchen."

"Come here!" exclaimed Chick Bronson in a tight voice.

Something made her drop her burden and hurry to him. Chick had wound up the length of well rope. Fastened to the hook at its end was, not a bucket, but a pair of brush-scarred, bulging saddle-bags.

She cried, "What on earth—?"

"Can't you guess?" He had the leather pouches unhooked and laid them out upon the well coping, and with fumbling hands was opening one of the flaps. From within the pouch he drew packets of paper— green, crisp banknotes.

He told her, "It's Ward McCarey's loot, of course— from the bank holdup at Three Pines!"

The wind, booming down the slope behind the ranch, caught at the edges of the bills and rattled them dryly. Josie took one of the packets in her hands, turned it over and over, staring at the money. It was all of high denominations and in fresh mint condition— protected by the leather pouches during these weeks it had hung, forgotten, in the dry well.

Suddenly she exclaimed, "I remember now! That day they took McCarey prisoner in our barn Grampa and I heard shooting and rode back to the ranch just as they were dragging him out, wounded and bloody. I felt sorry for him lying there like that—hurt. He was calling for water, and I took him a cup and held it for him while he drank.

"This is what I had forgotten until this minute. When he'd finished, he looked up at me and he tried to whisper something, but all I could make out of it was, 'The well—' I thought most likely he was out of his head with pain and trying to thank me for the water."

Chick Bronson nodded slowly. "McCarey had a sentimental streak in him that made him want to repay any kindness someone did for him while he was down. Just because I talked to him and kept him company, that night in jail, he gave me the only thing he had left to give—his lucky silver dollar. And yet I've sometimes wondered, in the back of my head, why it was he didn't think to tell me, instead, where this loot was buried. Especially when he knew he'd never have a chance to recover it himself."

He indicated the well. "This explains it. McCarey thought he had already given away the secret of the money to you—the price for that cup of water. He probably died happy in the belief that you and your grandfather were getting the good out of the money he had stolen."

Josie Freedom shook her head, her pretty face clouded with distress. "But what are we going to do with it? It will have to be returned, of course, and yet I don't think we dare trust Vince Kimbrough's sheriff enough to turn it over to him."

"That's the very last thing you'd want to do!" Chick

told her quickly. "Can't you see, it would play right into Kimbrough's hands! He could make real political copy of this! He could start folks thinking your grandfather had had the money from Ward McCarey, that he'd been holding it all this time, until finally it got too hot to handle and he had to be rid of it! Why, before he was through Kimbrough could make Matt Freedom out as big a crook as Ward McCarey himself. And where would be the chances for election then?"

Josie saw the danger, and it turned her quite pale. "Oh, Chick! Do you really think?"

"Yes, I do!" He took her by the shoulder, impulsively. "But maybe you'll trust *me,* Josie!" he exclaimed, searching her eyes. "Maybe you figure you know me well enough now that you'd dare depend on me to take care of this for you! Because there's a way out. If a grub-line rider's word is worth anything, I give you mine that this money will be turned over to the law, where it belongs, and that nobody need ever know Lazy F had anything to do with it!"

For a long minute he got no answer, and a leaden weight began to settle inside him. Of course she didn't trust him. What business had he supposing, for even a moment, that she could? He dropped his arm, turned away with a shrug.

"Thank you, Chick!"

He looked down, in slow amazement, as the packet of money she had been holding was confidingly placed in his hand. "I think I've learned to know you pretty well just today," she told him quietly. "I'm only hoping you won't run any risk to yourself doing this for Grampa and me!"

The leaden inner weight dissolved; his heart turned suddenly light. "Don't you worry, lady," he said. "I've got it all figured. There'll be no risk—I promise!" He added, "You go on and find your grandfather now, and just leave this to me!"

Minutes later he had the bills stuffed back into their pouches and the saddlebags slung into place behind his rig. With a final wave of the hand he rode away from the Lazy F; but at a short distance he pulled in for what he knew would likely be the last look he would ever have. He saw Josie Freedom, a small figure in saddle, heading away from the ranch buildings. He watched until he lost her in the rolling swells of the valley floor and the dust her pony had raised was a dim stain in the air that the ground wind quickly swept away.

A poignant knife of regret for the unfairness of things stabbed through him. If he only could have had something to offer a girl like that, instead of being what he was.

Such thoughts could get him nowhere, and he shrugged them aside. He nudged his sorrel forward, with the fifty thousand dollars that didn't belong to him slung behind his saddle.

TWENTY-THREE

A lone cottonwood, that scattered its few remaining golden leaves into the wind sweeping down from the valley rim, struck Chick Bronson as being right for his purposes. He dismounted and tied, and hunted about until he found a sturdy length of windfall that would be stout enough to dig with. The saddlebags slung over one shoulder then, he set his back to the tree, got his directions, and began pacing directly south from it, measuring his steps.

The count of fifty took him over the lip of an eroded wash and to a deep-sunk boulder that long-ago floods had carried down and deposited there. Wheeling, he sought a likely landmark along the broken north rim and finally chose a deep notch that somewhat resembled the rear leaf of a rifle's sights. Facing toward this, he again counted his steps moving at an angle now to his former course. At ten paces he had reached the bank of the wash again, and here, under the base of a stout clump of buckbrush, he started digging.

Using the crude shovel, he hollowed out a good-sized excavation in the crumbling cutbank, with the wind swirling about him and lifting the grit into his face and eyes. Before he was finished, he had discarded the heavy windbreaker. Finally throwing aside the stick, he sleeved sweat from his face and then picked up the saddlebags and tried the fit of them in the hole.

It was all right. Satisfied, he pulled them free, shook the loose dirt from them, slung them over his shoulder again. He turned to get his discarded windbreaker.

A voice said, "By God, I been watching this for ten minutes and I still don't know what he's up to!"

His head lifted with a jerk. On the bank of the wash, not a dozen feet away, stood a pair whose existence he had almost completely forgotten. He saw where their horses had been left, ground hitched; absorbed in his labor, he'd let them move in on top of him without noticing. Big Ed Dugan held a gun, dangling it carelessly. Ott Stanger merely stood with arms akimbo, a mocking look of triumph on his cruel face.

Stanger shook his head. "Damned if I make sense out of it either," he agreed. "It looked at first as though he meant to bury those saddlebags, but that don't rightly seem to have been the idea." He made a gesture of indifference. "Well, keep your eye on him, Ed. I'll relieve him of the loot, since he don't seem able to make up his mind what he wants to do with it!"

He came down the shallow bank of the draw, sending boot heels deep into the crumbling earth. There was nothing Chick Bronson could do to stop him as he snatched the heavy saddle pouches from his arm and with deft fingers ripped the flaps open, revealing the packets of money within.

Dugan called anxiously, "Is it there, boss?"

"It's here." Stanger favored the prisoner with his icy stare. "So, after all, we end the way we started! I knew, if we waited long enough, you'd finally lead us to this. I've had Dugan watching every move you made, waiting for you to grow confident enough to dig the money up—a nuisance, that way, but safer than trying to buck Vince Kimbrough a second time. And all the while the saddlebags were at Lazy F!"

Ed Dugan came scrambling down the bank now, still holding the gun. His mouth all but watered at sight of the bulging leather pouches. "You've sure as hell been leadin' me a chase!" he growled at Chick. "I told the boss when he rode over to check with me today that I was ready to quit. A good thing he made me hang on just an hour or two longer!"

Too sick inside to answer, Chick could only stare dismally at his captors. This time, he knew, they had the thing they were after, and no Bob Creel would appear at a fortuitous moment to catch them off their guard and set him free. Only his own wits could save him, and he had no confidence in those. Right now his mind was a hopeless blank.

"Incidentally," Ott Stanger demanded harshly, "what about the gun you took off me that night in the stable? I want that. Where is it?"

"The coat pocket," Chick said resignedly, indicating the discarded canvas windbreaker that lay in a heap a few yards distant. Stanger walked over and picked up the garment, to begin rummaging in its cavernous pockets.

Ed Dugan had the saddlebags slung across a forearm and with his free hand had pawed out a fistful of the packets of crisp green bills. He vented animal grunts

of pleasure as he examined them, brutish features lighted by his greed. Obviously it was the largest amount of money he had ever held in his fingers at one moment, and he was likely thinking less of what it could buy him—the clothes, the women, and the liquor—than of the mere feel of the money itself. Suddenly he commenced cramming the wads of bills into his clothing.

Ott Stanger said, "Put it back, Ed!"

His crisp order jolted the big man. Dugan lifted his head, looked at his boss stupidly. "There's plenty!"

"I said put it back!" Stanger's voice was sharp and cold. "You'll be paid your share later." Big Dugan's thick chest lifted with angry emotion. It didn't occur to him to disobey, however, and with the surly look of a scolded adolescent he shoved the money back into the pouch again.

Already quarreling over the spoils, Chick Bronson thought with tired disgust. With crooks like these it was what you could expect. It made this tainted money seem somehow more unclean than ever.

"Now put those bags down and keep away from them!" Ott Stanger told his bodyguard.

Dugan hesitated, scowling darkly. He was probably well used to receiving such curt tongue-lashings, but sight and feel of the loot must have wakened in him instincts of greed and a certain submerged yearning toward rebellion. Reluctantly he dumped the leather pouches to the ground at his feet. Standing over them, his bearlike shoulders rolled forward, he said thickly,

"Boss, I know we never discussed it, but I'm thinkin' we ought to cut this two ways—an even split."

"Even?" grunted Stanger, in cold scorn. "Why you big lunk! What do you think you'd ever do with that kind of cash?"

"Oh, I could spend it all right," the other insisted doggedly. "And I've had more'n my share of the trouble. I want what I've earned."

"You'll take what I give you! Now shut up and bring the horses!"

"But, boss—"

Stanger's voice was sharply dangerous. "I said shut up! Do as you're told or you may not get anything out of those saddlebags!"

The prisoner could see rebellion mounting high in Dugan, but the habit of obedience was long engrained and this habit won out. With a whine of self-pity the big man heeled about and went up the bank, digging his heavy boots into the earth, heading for the waiting pair of horses. Stanger, still hunting for his silver-handled gun, flipped the canvas jacket over and shoved his hand into the other pocket. Chick heard his grunt of satisfaction.

Throat suddenly dry, Chick waited until Stanger's hand came into view with the gun in it. And then he put everything into a quick and startling cry: "Dugan! *Look out!*"

Pulled around by the shout, big Dugan saw Stanger turning, holding a weapon. Nerves already tensed by argument brought Dugan's arm up in a convulsive,

unthinking movement, and the gun in Dugan's fingers leaped and thundered—directly at his boss.

To the shot Stanger went stumbling backward, only a quick scraping of boot sole against rubble keeping him on his feet. He stood like that, with his body drawn up and the red stain slowly spreading on his chest, and on his face a dumb look of surprise and incomprehension. He looked at Dugan; he looked down at the gun which he had made no move to fire. Then, shaking his head as though still not understanding, he opened his hand and let the gun drop to the dirt in front of him.

Afterward his knees broke and he spilled down in a twisting fall, to land upon the weapon.

In the silence of the fading gun echoes Ed Dugan's deep-drawn breath was a rasping sound. "Try to shoot me in the back, would he?" he croaked hoarsely. "Thanks for the warning, Bronson!"

Chick couldn't answer. Now that the thing was done, Chick knew a shakiness in all his limbs so that he had to stiffen his knees to stay erect. It hadn't been anything thought out or planned—merely a wild, half-reasoning instinct that had told him to shout, knowing Dugan was so wrought up that sight of Stanger with a naked gun in his hand might be enough to start the gunman shooting wildly. It had been a trick, and a peculiarly unclean one. But it had lost him one of his foes.

One was still alive, however, and still dangerous.

Dugan came shuffling back into the draw. He put a

heavy boot toe under Stanger's body, nudged him, and let him fall back limply. He seemed oddly at a loss. He was used to taking orders; and being left suddenly on his own, without anyone to tell him what to do, he hardly appeared to know what his next move ought to be. But then he remembered the saddlebags, and he went and picked them up, and looked over at Chick. He still held the smoking gun.

"I dunno," he muttered uncertainly. "I kind of hate to shoot a man that's saved my life—even you, Bronson. But Ott said it wasn't safe to let you go."

Desperately Chick tried to reassure him. "You don't have to be afraid of me! I don't want any of the money—I don't want to have anything more to do with it! I'll get on my bronc and you'll never see or hear of me again."

"No!" Dugan shook his big head stubbornly. He had absorbed Stanger's warning, and it had become an unshakable tenet of belief with him that Chick Bronson must die. The weapon lifted in his hand, its muzzle a great black threat pointed squarely at the helpless victim's face.

"This is the most money I ever see," he grunted. "I ain't takin' no chances."

Chick felt the sting of sweat breaking out upon him. "Don't be a fool!" he cried. "You can't spend it anyway!"

"Why not?" The gun wavered slightly, something in Chick's sharp words penetrating the other's slow brain.

"Didn't you take a good look at it? Most of those bills are mint condition, never circulated. Beyond any doubt in the world the serial numbers have been posted with every bank in the country. You try passing that stuff and see how quick the law pounces on you!"

It was a new idea to Dugan, obviously. He blinked once as it sunk home, then with an oath he pawed open one of the leather pockets, dragged out a handful of bills, and squinted at the numbers. His face darkened with fury and disappointment. "There must be some way—" he mumbled.

"Sure there's a way. Stanger would have known what to do, but you haven't got his connections. And if you tried asking questions, first thing you know you'd have talked to the wrong man and he'd deal you out and take it all away from you.

"There's dynamite in those saddlebags, Dugan! Better not play around with it if you don't savvy what you're doing. I'll tell you, though," he added, as an afterthought, "if you want me to I'll take the money off your hands and turn it over to the law for you, and you won't have to answer any embarrassing questions—"

He had pressed too hard. He saw Dugan's doubts settle into stubbornness, his ugly face go bleak. The hand tightened on the gun. "Like hell you will! I ain't giving this up to you, or to the law, or anybody, until I've found out for sure there's no way to make it pay off. I'll burn the stuff first! And I'll kill you or any other man that gets in my road!"

Chick dragged in a deep breath. "All right, Dugan," he said. "You win! Put the gun away and I'll show you the only chance you have of cashing in—not for fifty thousand, of course, but enough anyhow to make it worth your while. It means me selling out the people at Lazy F, but a man's life is worth more than promises."

The big fellow looked dubious. "*Now* what's on your mind?" he demanded harshly.

"Put away the gun first. I can't talk with it staring me in the face."

He waited, trying to appear adamant and self-certain; and at last, after a long and chilling minute, Ed Dugan lowered the gun. He even stabbed it into its holster, but he kept his huge paw wrapped around the butt. "Well?" he snarled dangerously.

Something of the tightness eased a little in Chick. He plunged ahead with his proposition.

"You wondered what I was up to when you caught me with those saddlebags just now. I wasn't burying them—I was trying to arrange things to back up my story, later, when I turned them over to the law and said that McCarey had given me the directions for locating his cache. I didn't ever want it known that the money was actually hidden on the Lazy F—not with Vince Kimbrough gunning for the Freedoms."

Ed Dugan scowled. "I dunno nothin' about all this. Vince Kimbrough is sure as hell no friend of mine!"

"He could be, if you took this money to him and told him it came out of the Freedoms' well! Take my word for it, Dugan. Because of what this could mean for him, politically, he'd make it plenty well worth your trouble! And he'd be a good man for you to hook up with, permanent, now that Ott Stanger's through."

"Kimbrough wouldn't even give me a chance to tell my story! I so much as stick my nose in his town, and he'd sick that Bob Creel on me!"

"No, he wouldn't. That's where I come in. I'll make him listen! I put you in touch with Kimbrough, and you forget about throwing a bullet into me. Is that a fair bargain?"

But Dugan's face was still dark with angry suspicion. "You must think I was born day before yesterday! All you're tryin' to do is talk me into lettin' myself be led into a trap!"

"That's that, then." Chick lifted his shoulders resignedly, "if you don't like my idea. It was the best I could manage—for both of us!"

An agony of indecision settled plainly on the big man. He could see all his cherished hopes for this loot of Ward McCarey's glimmering away to nothing, and himself left now without even a job, Stanger being dead. Dugan wasn't a man to face that prospect calmly. He was one who needed to take orders—needed a stronger mind and personality than his own to lend him the comforting security of a sure job and definite work to do.

His ugly little eyes glared at Chick; his maul-like hands twitched.

"All right!" he blurted. "I'll have to take a chance.

But, boy, I'm warning you! If this ain't on the level—
if I see one single thing that don't look right—I'll burn
you down and ask questions afterward! You'll never
spring the trap and live—understand? So if you don't
mean to play square with me, you better forget it right
now!"

Chick Bronson met his look squarely. "Fair enough.
I'm ready to ride any time you are."

TWENTY-FOUR

There was not much light left in the day when they
came into Lost Wolf, and lamps already burned in
some of the houses. A pair of riders drifting in with the
evening did not make a particularly noticeable sight,
but Ed Dugan seemed nervous as a cat; Vince Kimbrough's town was dangerous territory for him, and he
rode alongside Chick with a busy glance roving the
darkening streets and a thick hand hitched close to his
gun.

Chick watched that hand, himself uneasy enough.
He knew that Dugan was geared to instant action, and
if anything happened to start him digging for gun
metal it would be Chick Bronson himself who would
draw the first bullet. Dugan had meant that for a
promise.

But the streets were almost deserted, and silent.
Coming to the small frame building that housed Kimbrough's land company office, they saw the lamp
burning inside and the aged clerk on his high stool,

working at the desk. They dismounted and tied; Dugan took down the saddlebags, slung them over an arm. He motioned Chick ahead of him, across the plank walk; at his command Chick pushed the door open.

"Where's your boss?" he asked the clerk who twisted about on his stool.

He thought there was something odd in the way the latter stared at him before giving answer. "Not here. Over at the Bull's Head, I think."

"Get Kimbrough here," Dugan ordered in a whisper. "And alone!"

Chick cleared his throat. "Would you fetch him for me? Tell him I got important news that he'll want to hear. And it might be better if he came by himself."

With Dugan watching, he didn't dare attempt to signal a warning that all was not as it should be. Even so, the clerk was eying him strangely, and for a moment Chick thought he would decline to carry the message; finally he laid aside his pen and slid down off the stool, and without a word took hat and coat from a wall peg. They stood aside for him as he scurried through the door, heading for the saloon across the street.

Dugan's nervousness seemed on the increase. He at once began a quick tour of the narrow room, pulling shades, and even trying the rear door for a look into the alley. Then he returned to the front window, waiting there in high tension for Vince Kimbrough to show in the street outside.

A grunt of satisfaction broke from him finally as he peered past the drawn shade. "Comin'!" he said. "And alone, all right." Yet he still fingered the butt of his gun.

Presently Kimbrough's steps were heard hitting the sidewalk and then the door was thrown open. Framed in it, the boss of Lost Wolf stood looking at his visitors.

Chick Bronson had let himself into a chair beside the main desk that stood next to a shade-drawn window. Kimbrough's stare slid off him, moved to the other man; it considered Dugan for a long moment, then turned again to Chick. "What is this all about, Bronson?"

He would have given much not to have had to answer. He had stalled, up until this moment, by every desperate means—even risking the welfare of the Freedoms in order to gain time and a chance at escape. But this chance had failed to present itself, and now that the pay-off had arrived, Chick was appalled to see the irremediable damage he had done in his panicky effort to save his own neck.

He said miserably, "Dugan's got something he wants to talk to you about, boss. A deal."

"Oh?" Frowning, Kimbrough closed the door behind him and walked into the room. He circled the desk, opened a box of cigars and, taking one, rolled it between his fingertips as he studied Dugan's ugly face. "This has something to do with Ott Stanger, I suppose?"

Dugan shook his head. "If the kid here has been tellin' me straight, what I got to sell is a lot more important to you than Stanger."

Taking his time about it, Vince Kimbrough lifted the cigar to his lips and bent to turn the flame of the lamp higher while he got a light at the mouth of the glass chimney. Looking at that gaunt face, with its deep-carved lines and somber mouth shadowed now by the upward spray of lamp glow, Chick had to remind himself of the things he had come to know about this man. You would have thought that the heartless greed which motivated him should reveal itself somewhere in the mask he wore; yet even now Chick could find in it nothing but a sad and thoughtful earnestness.

Kimbrough straightened, the cigar alight and drawing. "Well!" he grunted. "You've got something to sell me, have you?" His voice altered, gone suddenly harsh and rimmed with sarcasm. "Ott Stanger's gunman! And Bronson, here, who of course has my interests at heart. It's only natural that you'd try and arrange to get me alone."

Chick Bronson's spine felt a touch of icy chill at what he heard, thinly concealed, in Kimbrough's voice. Even Dugan seemed to sense that something had gone wrong; he was scowling uncertainly, head thrust forward, mean eyes pinned to Kimbrough's face.

"Why, this is kind of a private matter," mumbled Dugan. "We don't want the whole world in on it!"

"I'm sure you don't!" The mockery of the other's

tone had mounted till it touched his brooding stare. "Sorry!" he said. "But I have to do things my own way." And then, lifting his voice sharply, "All right, Bob!"

At his summons the alley door swung open under the drive of a boot toe that sent it slamming into the wall. In the opening, face disfigured by the swollen marks of Chick Bronson's fists, a gun leveled in his hand, stood Bob Creel.

Chick understood everything then. The possibility somehow hadn't occurred to him that Creel could find a horse and get here ahead of him, to report what had happened out on the trail. No wonder, then, the clerk had stared! No wonder that Kimbrough, on being told of Chick's audacity in showing himself again in this town, had brought Bob Creel along with him!

But now Ed Dugan's startled oath reminded Chick of another forgotten peril. For, yonder, Dugan had finally broken free of the first shock and now his big head was swiveling, angry eyes hunting for Chick Bronson. In Dugan's slow brain all this could have but one meaning. He had been betrayed—and he had given plenty warning what would happen should anything go wrong.

Hardly even thinking, Chick started for the floor and the poor protection of the bulky desk. Even as he was falling, Dugan shot; the bullet, reaching for Chick's moving figure, chanced to strike the lamp instead. He flinched as hot, splintered glass and burning oil sprayed him, but with it a grateful darkness descended upon the room—a darkness made complete by the drawn window shades that kept out any possible filtering of street light.

Straight on the heels of the first shot came a second, from a gun stationed by the rear door. Dimly Chick realized Bob Creel was targeting the flash of Dugan's weapon—thinking, no doubt, that Dugan's bullet had been meant for him. Over and over the guns spoke, stabbing their lances of fire and mingling an ear-punishing racket upon the close air of the room, while Chick Bronson, unarmed and helpless, hugged the floor and waited out the storm.

Dugan's cry of agony ended it as abruptly as it had begun. The gunfire ceased. There was the fall of a heavy body, and then, through pulsing gun echoes, Vince Kimbrough's hoarse shout: "One down, Bob! Now get the other one; get that Bronson devil—"

There was one chance. The window in the wall behind him was closed, probably locked. But in desperate haste Chick whirled and grabbed the chair in which he had sat and hurled it at the window. It crashed through, taking wood and glass and shade. And he followed in a reckless dive.

He hit the ground, amid the litter of broken window, with almost force enough to knock the wind out of his body. Though dazed, he still had the urgency of self-preservation to bring him stumbling to his feet, for he heard now the pound of boots within as Creel and his master charged the window, cursing the furniture they stumbled against in the dark.

Seeking flight, Chick thought first of his horse, tied out in front of the office, and he turned along the side of the building in that direction. Almost at once, however, he checked himself. Others were coming that way; he could hear the scuff of running boots, and a voice he thought belonged to the sheriff yelled, "What's going on? You having trouble, Kimbrough?"

"It's Bronson!" answered Kimbrough's shout within the office. "He just killed a man. Don't let him reach his horse. Bob, you get out the back way in case he breaks for the alley!"

Blocked, Chick halted just short of the building corner and wheeled, thinking to try an escape toward the rear before Creel had time to cut him off. But next moment he had to hurl himself flat against the clapboard siding, for Vince Kimbrough had thrust head and shoulders through the shattered window a couple yards or so from where he stood.

He sucked in breath, trying to weld himself there so the other man couldn't line up his profile against the dim light of the street beyond. And now running men were coming past him round the corner of the building, so close that their clothing all but brushed his own.

"Didn't head that way, Kimbrough!"

"The alley, then. But leave a guard to watch his horse."

"I already did," the sheriff answered, and to his followers: "Come on, come on! Let's move!" It occurred to Chick that Mart Murray seemed pretty spry for a man supposedly just recovered from a smashed hip. Probably that, too, had all been part of the trap they'd laid for old Matt Freedom, with Chick himself as the bait.

Murray had nearly a dozen with him. And as they went past Chick, their boots spurting cinders against his legs, he saw a single risky chance to get out of this predicament. Suddenly pushing away from his hiding place, he fell into stride and went with them through the darkness, past the window where Vince Kimbrough was leaning out to wave them on.

Back in the alley, they bunched up briefly as the sheriff halted for a puzzled word with Bob Creel, who had arrived ahead of them. "Damned if I know where he went!" Creel said. "Not a sign of him here. He must have been moving blamed fast!"

"We'd have spotted him, sure, did he cut toward the street!" Murray insisted.

By this time Vince Kimbrough had come hurrying from the rear door of the office building. "Talking won't find him!" he snapped impatiently. "Split up the men. Leave a couple here in case he doubles back, and the rest of us will try both ends of the alley. If we don't cross his trail by then we'll have to start searching the houses. Because I want that man, Sheriff—whether dead or alive, it doesn't matter which! I want him!"

TWENTY-FIVE

"Right, boss!" Mart Murray started shouting orders. "You men heard that—the guy's a killer, and we aren't letting him get away. You"—his finger stabbed the air twice, the second time straight at Chick Bronson— "and you! Watch for him here, and keep your eyes peeled! The rest—start moving!"

In another second or two he had the bunch of men halved and they were hurrying off, down either wing of the long, back alley.

So many things were happening so fast that Chick could feel his head spinning, his tight-stretched nerves making leaps that sent spasms of chill coursing his sweaty, trembling body. He tried to force himself under control as he stood there in deep shadows with the face of that other man who had been left behind making a dim blob not far from him. It seemed to him that the pounding of his own heart must drown out every other noise of the night.

His companion said suddenly, "Aw, hell! They'll never catch him!"

Chick shot him a glance. Seeing that the other was looking at him, he tried to draw farther back into the shadows. He didn't dare betray himself by speaking.

"They let him through their hands," the man continued. "He'll find a horse and be out of town while they're still beating the alleys! Right?" This time he waited for a reply and, getting none, asked another question. "Any idea who it was the guy's supposed to have killed?"

Forced to answer, Chick managed a muffled "No!" and then held his breath, waiting. But his companion seemed to notice nothing, and time dragged on for another minute, broken by the distant sounds of the man hunters calling back and forth along the alley.

"Aw, the hell with it!" the man grunted, in sudden disgust. And he snapped a match for the cigarette he had stuffed between his lips.

"Put that out!" cried Chick hoarsely. But the glow of the light had already touched his face, and before he could reach the man's arm to bat the match out of his hand, he knew he had been recognized.

"Say! Ain't you—?"

Chick hit him, his knuckles merely grazing the beard stubble of the other's flat jaw. A warning squawk broke from the man. "It's Bronson! Hey, Sheriff!" Then, desperately, Chick struck again, and this time his blow hit home.

He felt the head jerk back under his fist, heard the solid thud as it bounced hard against the wall. That was really what put the fellow out. He slid limply down, and the gun he had started to pull went spinning out of his fingers, to clatter somewhere among cinders.

No time to hunt for it. Already, from either end of the alley, the man hunters were returning in full cry. Chick speared an anxious look about him as he flexed his numb right hand to work the feeling back into it.

And then, because he had to have a hiding place quick, he picked the only one he saw.

There was a rain barrel below the rear corner of Kimbrough's flat-roofed one-storied office building. Chick crossed to it, leaped to a precarious balance on the rim. The barrel threatened to topple, righted itself. Then, chafing his hands on tar-paper roofing, he pulled himself up, got his elbows under him, and with a convulsive movement wriggled atop the building and flopped there prone. And none too quickly.

Almost immediately the alley below seemed to be swarming with men. He lay and listened to them, heard Vince Kimbrough demanding to know who had called out, and what had become of the pair he stationed here.

About this time someone stumbled over the man Chick Bronson had hit. He was already recovering. They got him roused and in a few minutes had the story from him.

"Come on!" yelled Kimbrough. "He's somewhere right under our noses! Find him, wherever he is! Don't let him get to a horse. Don't let him leave this town. I want that killer!"

A voice Chick knew belonged to Bob Creel said savagely, "You don't want him any more than I do! If I ever just get my hands on him . . ."

The man hunt continued. It had fanned out now to cover the entire town, with scarcely a man who wasn't spurred to take part. And Chick Bronson, spread flat on the office roof with the night wind whipping coldly at him, wondered bleakly just what his chances were. He had crawled to the forward edge of the roof, peering over in time to watch his sorrel and Ed Dugan's horse being led away somewhere for safe-keeping. They intended making sure of him all right. All the scattered hitch racks had been cleared, the horses collected and placed under guard.

He watched the dark figures of armed men moving through the town, going from house to house now, probing every shed and cellarway where a man might hide. Others had mounted and ridden to circle and try to pick up his trail, in case he attempted to sneak away on foot. One rider was sent spurring out of town on the west trail, clattering briefly over the planks of the bridge: Chick guessed that that one must be heading toward Box K to bring reinforcements from the bunkhouse crew.

Nobody, apparently had thought to try the roof-tops; but no telling when they might think of it.

The best part of an hour dragged out; the search seemed to have passed its height of activity, begun to simmer down. Sooner or later, he thought desperately, they were bound to relax their vigilance enough for him to sneak down from his perch. Otherwise, the coming of daylight would eventually betray him.

All he asked now was a chance to be free of this town and this valley and the grief they had meant to him. Lying there, scared and bone-chilled by the wind, he went over it all in his mind—back to its beginnings in the jailhouse where Ward McCarey had slipped him a doomed silver dollar and gone out to his death. Now Ott Stanger was dead, and big Dugan. And that cursed dollar was still in his pocket.

He ought to have flung it away long ago. Not only had it given him no good luck, but it had brought misery to himself and to the Freedoms—had even cost him his old sorrel cowpony and, before the night was ended, perhaps his life as well.

He had reached this point in his bleak musings when he heard Kimbrough and Bob Creel return together and enter the office below him.

Through the roof timbers the sounds of their moving about were plain down there, while voices came as an indistinct rumbling. Once, when Creel stumbled against some piece of furniture in the dark, Chick caught his angry words. Shortly after this he judged that Kimbrough had located a new lamp and got it burning.

The droning voices continued sporadically, and then, suddenly, came the thing he had been waiting for—the startled exclamation that told him the saddle-bags under Ed Dugan's body had been discovered and opened. "Look, boss!" he heard Bob Creel yell out, quite distinctly. "Look at the bank wrappers! It's what McCarey—!"

"Not so loud, you fool!" rapped Kimbrough. Their voices dropped away again, but the listener could tell they were talking rapidly and with a fierce intensity. And little wonder! That was a good piece of money for any man to have drop into his lap—even one of

Kimbrough's stature. He, of course, would know of a way to use it, despite the telltale serial numbers.

And so, after all the men who had died for it—the bank clerk at Three Pines, McCarey himself, Stanger, Dugan—the money was at last to end in the greedy hands of Vince Kimbrough. Not only that, it gave added reason why one man more must die, for Kimbrough would be doubly concerned now that Chick Bronson be put out of the way, so as to preserve the secret.

It was while Chick was trying with renewed effort to catch some hint of what went on in that room below him that he became aware of a new sound blanketing the hum of voices, growing momentarily stronger. He lifted his head and saw the riders as they moved slowly into sight along the street.

He blinked, and stared again. For so many riders, they came with little noise or confusion. There were nearly two dozen, he thought—hard to count exactly in the occasional glow of windows as they drifted past. But he saw a face or two he recognized, and startled understanding filled in the rest.

Leading the rest were Martin Talbot and old Matt Freedom. These were the Pool ranchers and their crews.

Up there on the roof, with the harsh wind whipping at him, Chick Bronson watched them pull rein at a signal from Talbot's upraised hand. Spread out, they nearly filled the wide street. Restless horses stamped and blew, with a rattling of bit chains here and there.

Lamplight touched up glints of brightness that Chick knew must mean short guns and rifles, openly carried.

A word spoken to quiet a horse sounded once or twice; while in the forefront Talbot and Freedom and one or two other leaders were holding hurried counsel, pointing now and then at the office building where lamplight showed behind the drawn blind of the front window.

Suddenly Martin Talbot spurred his mount forward, and he called sharply into the stillness, "All right, Kimbrough! If you're there, step out!"

The buzz of voices beneath Chick sheared off abruptly. Here and there doors and windows began to slam open; a few men drifted out onto porches and under the tin-roofed arcades that fronted along the street. But none of these ventured farther, and from the land company office itself there was no sound at all for long moments.

Then boots strode heavily forward and the door was flung open, laying a pattern of lamplight over the ground before it. Centering this was the long shadow of Vince Kimbrough. It flowed out across the plank sidewalk, across the ruts of the roadway. And then Bob Creel stepped through the door after his boss, quickly moving to one side.

Coming cautiously to his elbows, Chick Bronson found he could look directly down on that pair of foreshortened figures; but he himself apparently remained unnoticed, as yet, by anyone below.

"Well? I'm here!" said Kimbrough, laying his voice

across the windy, shadow-clotted street. "Who calls my name?"

Martin Talbot answered him loudly, "The members of the Pool! Can you guess why we've come? It's because we're fed up—fed up and ready for a settlement!"

"Don't you realize you're talking foolishness?" Kimbrough's voice held a weary patience that might have deceived Chick Bronson twenty-four hours ago. "You merely want someone you can blame for your troubles—a way of letting off steam, after nursing personal grievances too long without any kind of release.

"I've done nothing to you! Your troubles are economic and nationwide. Go on home and think it over; you'll see that I'm talking sense!"

"You can't put us off with words!" retorted Talbot. "If we're fools, it's for not having done this before! It's for thinking we could settle our score with you in any other way!"

"Just step out of the saddle, Talbot!" Bob Creel challenged. "If you're so hot on settling something—"

"No!"

Kimbrough flung an arm across his gunman's chest, to hold him back. "There's already been enough violence!" he cried. "My God! Can't we act like reasonable men? Just what is it you people think you want with me?"

"To run you out of town, Kimbrough!" somebody in the mass of riders shouted back. "And clean off this range."

Martin Talbot had piled his hands on the saddle horn; he leaned forward upon them, looking straight at Kimbrough across the acrid dust. "We took a vote," he said quietly. "After what we learned today, we're agreed there's nothing else left us."

"And may I ask what it was you learned?"

"Just the schemes you cooked up to discredit our candidate in the election next week! Tax frauds and robbery and murder. You were stopped there; but if we let it go you'll try some other trick—and maybe that time you'll get away with it. We aren't going to give you the chance. This is showdown!"

TWENTY-SIX

Kimbrough's voice was rough-edged with suppressed anger. "Where did you hear anything as fantastic as this—if you didn't make it up out of whole cloth?"

"We got it from a good source: from one of your own men—Bronson!"

"Bronson!" The name was spat out scornfully. "That cheap crook! He took me in, too, with his lies—took me in so well that I gave the grub-liner a job and even got him work collecting taxes for the sheriff. It wasn't till today that I found out he's been falsifying his collection and pocketing the difference. Naturally I fired him—gave him an hour to quit the valley. And this is how he gets back at me: He tells you these lies, and then sneaks back into town to try and kill me himself!"

A gasp broke from the man who listened, unseen in the darkness of the roof, to this vilification. He might even have lost his head right then had it not been for the quiet answer spoken by old Matt Freedom.

"We counted on you giving us some such yarn. I reckon we'll stick with Bronson's version!"

Vince Kimbrough must have known, then, that talking had failed. Yet what he said, after the briefest of pauses, was, "I tell you what. We'll never accomplish anything this way. Why don't we step across the street to the Bull's Head and all have a drink—on me, of course. Surely we can work this thing out."

And Chick knew what the man was doing—stalling desperately. Even though Lost Wolf was his town, Kimbrough could not hope too much for help from those who watched in the shadows along the street; not even Mart Murray could do a lot against such odds. Kimbrough's real strength lay in the guns of the Box K, and Chick remembered suddenly how he had seen a rider leaving town an hour earlier, heading across the river. Kimbrough must figure that if he could keep these others talking long enough, the arrival of Spud Lantry and the crew would tip the balance.

He was not going to manage this, however, for Martin Talbot turned in the saddle, and he was telling his followers: "I don't think we need any of this gent's whisky! It wouldn't be polite to drink with him just before we run him out of town."

"Hell, no!" someone echoed. "Let's get on with what we come for!"

And as a stirring went through them, Vince Kimbrough turned and spoke softly to his henchman—but not so softly that the man on the edge of the roof failed to hear every word. "Get their leader! Get Talbot, and get him good! Then we'll duck inside and hold off the rest until help comes!"

There was no time to think or to weigh the danger. Martin Talbot was still twisted about on his horse, unaware what went on behind him. And as Bob Creel's gun slid smoothly from holster, Chick Bronson, without a weapon, came up quickly to his heels and launched himself in a flat dive straight off the edge of the roof.

A startled yell from someone was the only warning Creel got. Then Chick's full weight hit him solidly, and he went down, absorbing most of the shock. Even so, Chick had some of the wind knocked out of him, and he lay there dazed and gasping, to become gradually aware that the man beneath him had begun to struggle.

The shouting of the crowd seemed to pour in upon his ears at the same moment—like the releasing of a dike. He stirred himself, collected his strength. Bob Creel was really fighting now, trying hard to buck him off, but not as yet with a great deal of steam. Chick cursed and put all he had into a clubbing, chopping blow that he drove at the back of the man's neck.

It was enough. All the fight ran out of Creel, and he collapsed—so completely and suddenly that Chick lost balance and had to catch himself by stabbing a hand against the sidewalk planking.

Crouched like that, he lifted his head. Bob Creel's six-shooter lay in the dirt just beyond the sidewalk, where it had slid as it fell from the gunman's hand. Chick went for it. The edge of the planking struck his chest and then he was groping, scrabbling in the dirt in an effort to get his fingers on the weapon. And it was then that the other gun spoke, and a skewer of white-hot fire burnt its way into Chick Bronson's thigh.

His whole body jerked to the drive of the bullet. Through sweat and bullet shock he peered upward — straight into the muzzle of Vince Kimbrough's smoking six-shooter and into Kimbrough's face.

All the hypocrisy was missing from that face. It was twisted, angry, vengeful; ugly with his hatred of this grub-line rider who had spelled the ruin of his scheming. Everything else appeared to have been forgotten, except his eagerness to see Chick Bronson's death. And it was obvious, too, that the Pool men were themselves too much in the grip of surprise for them to move quickly enough to interfere.

Chick sensed this dimly, and the need to save himself kept him going. He got his fingers closed on the fallen gun somehow, and he brought it up, though it seemed to weigh a tremendous amount. The hammer resisted him as he fought it back into cock. It took all his strength to tilt the muzzle upward and to work the trigger.

He never knew for certain whether Kimbrough got off a second bullet or not, but he did feel the kick of his own shot, slamming the revolver butt against his palm. Moments later, when he heard old Matt Freedom's anxious voice and felt hands upon him, lifting him, he had presence of mind to murmur thickly: "Get the saddlebags out of the office. Hold on to them. Don't let anything—happen to them." From a great distance he seemed to hear his voice saying it.

The bunk room at the Lazy F was a pleasant place these days, with the yellow November sunlight that flooded through the windows and the warm, rich smells from the kitchen swimming there. Josie Freedom had managed to learn all of Chick's favorite dishes and the kind of pie he liked best, and she kept the big wood range busy just turning them out.

It really wasn't quite fair, Chick felt, to treat a man that way—an invalid who couldn't help himself but whose hurts were fast mending so that he would soon have to be riding away and leaving all this behind him—taking with him only the memory of a girl with music in her voice and warm brown eyes—a girl he couldn't have. But he kept these thoughts and feelings, naturally, to himself.

They saw little of Matt these days; the newly elected county judge had his hands full enough in town, what with the breakup of Vince Kimbrough's range empire and the new broom that was being used to sweep all of Kimbrough's crooked hirelings clean out of the county courthouse. Maybe Freedom savvied little of book law but what he didn't know he made up for with rigid honesty and native common sense; and not only did his frail body bear up under this pressure of work but seemed actually to thrive under it, developing surprising reserves of strength. His color and spirits had never been better.

One particular afternoon he and Martin Talbot rode out from town together, and in the barn Matt found Chick Bronson going over his riding gear. Chick still limped some, but as he could at last sit saddle again he had forced himself to ride a little every day. Now there was a certain purposefulness about his actions that told old Matt what was in his mind. Hitching to a seat on the edge of an oat-bin, Matt said quietly, "Figuring to leave us?"

Chick nodded, not looking at him. "Yeah," he said. "Tomorrow."

"Josie know about it?"

"No, I wasn't going to tell her—thought she might argue. I'm well enough to ride, though, and I can't stay on here forever. I got to be finding me a job before winter hits."

The way Matt watched him checking the stitching of a cinch buckle, he appeared in no great hurry to answer, yet it was plain that he had something on his mind and was only holding back, savoring the excitement of what he had to tell.

"Interesting news in town today," he drawled finally, his mild eyes twinkling. "Seems the beef market in Kansas City and Chicago has done taken a tilt upward. Nothing much yet, still, the experts say it's the bottom of the trough. Come spring, anyway, and things ought to be on the upturn."

"That's fine," agreed Chick, but somehow with no real enthusiasm. "It's fine for all of us."

Matt continued, nodding, his eyes on Chick while he settled back comfortably with bony hands wrapped about one knee, "Yes, come spring, and with no Kimbrough around to keep us all in hot water, things on the Lost Wolf should look better than they ever have. We ought to be able to put a crew in that bunk room again and start running some cattle.

"For right now there's a lot that needs doing, to get ready. And my hands are pretty full with the job in town. What I'm getting at," he finished bluntly, "is that I wish you'd stick around, Bronson, and kind of take charge of the place!"

Chick lifted his head to stare at him. "You honestly mean that?"

"Sure. You're a good man that wants a job; I got a job that wants a man. And there's no man I'd rather have than you!"

The old man waited, his face smiling and warm with pleasure, but Chick Bronson did not answer him at once. Slowly he straightened from his work. He walked over to the doorway and leaned there looking into the yard, with the bleak November sunlight on him. "Sorry," he said finally. "I appreciate this. But I can't stay."

"What!" The old man came off the box in a hurry, stunned. "What do you mean you can't?"

"Lost Wolf River has been nothing but bad luck from the day I hit it." Chick's tone was dull, the words coming out of him jerkily. "It's nice country, but a man can generally tell when a place is jinxed for him. I've long decided I'd best get out as soon as I was able to stick to a saddle. My mind's made up.

"Damn it, you don't make sense!" exclaimed the old man, angry now. But by then he had come up in back of the younger man and, past Chick's elbow, could see the pair who stood talking earnestly out there in the yard beside the abandoned well—Josie and Martin Talbot. The girl's face was tilted up, very close to his, and Talbot's strong hand lay upon her arm.

When Matt spoke again, it was in a changed voice; there was understanding in him. He said quietly, "You haven't been telling me your real reasons, have you?"

Chick Bronson stiffened. Then, going loose again, he said gruffly, "No. I ain't!" And not looking at the old man again, he pulled away from the door and headed for the house with a purposeful stride.

In the bunk room he slammed the door, dropped down onto the edge of his bed, and scowled at the worn floor boards, as though he might find his troubled thoughts written there. His fingers, digging in a pocket, happened to come upon the battered shape of Ward McCarey's lucky dollar. He brought it out, looked at the pit of brightness where a bullet had once struck, and with a sudden, convulsive gesture flung it from him, to roll from sight beneath a wall bunk on the other side of the room.

"Better if I had never laid eyes on the damn thing," he grunted bleakly.

After that he went down on hands and knees and dragged the saddle roll from under his bunk. Unfastening the straps, he spread the blankets out and began putting away in them the few odds and ends of personal belongings that he had about the room, leaving out only his new, long-shanked razor and the clothing he would wear next day. He had the roll assembled and was pulling the straps tight when Josie Freedom's knock sounded at the door.

She entered at his call, and saw what he had been up to. Her face was clouded. "Grampa said you were leaving. It's true then?"

"True enough. High time I pulled out, I figure."

Josie didn't look at him, only at the neatly rolled blankets; it was as though she didn't want to see what was in his brooding eyes—or show him what lay in hers. She said in a low voice, "Don't you like—like us?"

"Maybe it's a question," he told her flatly, "of likin' too well. Likin' something I can't have!"

"And so you mean to run away from it—as you ran away from that Ozark farm you once told me about!"

He scowled. "It's not the same thing at all." Giving the bedroll strap a savage pull, he told himself he didn't want to lose his temper with her.

This time she did look at him. "Oh, isn't it?" she challenged. "You big, strong men—you'll stand up to a dozen gunmen, to show how brave you are, but when your personal affairs get out of hand you'd rather run from them any time! It's like I told Martin Talbot just now—"

"Let's keep Martin Talbot out of this!"

"—when he said for the last time if I wouldn't marry him he was going to sell his ranch and leave this valley. Men are all like that, I told him—unreasonable! Expecting, I suppose, that a girl can help it who she falls in love with."

She turned away before he could half-credit the meaning he thought he read in her eyes and voice. But then, choking out her name, Chick went limping after her and caught up with her in the doorway. She turned, smiling, her arms already opening to him.

"Josie!" he cried thickly. "Golly, I—I—"

There was no need to finish. For she stood tall, and with arms thrown around his neck brought his mouth down to meet her warm kiss. And Chick's own arms seemed to know right then, by instinct, just where they both should be.

Center Point Publishing
600 Brooks Road ● PO Box 1
Thorndike ME 04986-0001 USA

(207) 568-3717

US & Canada:
1 800 929-9108
www.centerpointlargeprint.com